GIOVANNA'S NAVEL
AND FOUR MORE STORIES

Ernest van der Kwast is a Dutch author born in Mumbai, India, in 1981. He made his debut in 2005 with the novel *Sometimes Things Are Better When People Applaud*. His breakthrough book is *Mama Tandoori*, which became a bestseller in the Netherlands and Italy upon publication, and has to date sold more than 100,000 copies. *Giovanna's Navel* is the third of his books (after *The Ice-Cream Makers* and *Mama Tandoori*) to be published in English. He lives in Rotterdam.

Giovanna's Navel
and four more stories

Ernest van der Kwast

Translated from the Dutch
by Laura Vroomen

SCRIBE
Melbourne · London

Scribe Publications
18–20 Edward St, Brunswick, Victoria 3056, Australia
2 John St, Clerkenwell, London, WC1N 2ES, United Kingdom

First published in Dutch by De Bezige Bij, Amsterdam 2012
First published in English by Scribe 2018

Printed and bound in the UK by CPI Group (UK) Ltd, Croydon, CR0 4YY

Scribe Publications is committed to the sustainable use of natural resources
and the use of paper products made responsibly from those resources.

9781925322958 (Australian edition)
9781911617051 (UK edition)
9781925548686 (e-book)

Nederlands
letterenfonds
dutch foundation
for literature
This publication has been made possible with
financial support from the Dutch Foundation
for Literature.

CiP records for this title are available from the British Library and the
National Library of Australia and British Library.

scribepublications.com.au
scribepublications.co.uk

Contents

Giovanna's Navel

It was the most beautiful day in the postman's life. His phone began to beep and buzz just as he pushed a white envelope through the letterbox of Number 5b. Before it had even dropped onto the wooden floor behind the door, the postman had pressed the phone to his ear and heard his wife crying, 'They're on their way! Our little sweethearts are on their way!'

A tear welled up in his left eye and for a moment the postman didn't know what to say. He'd known this day would come — for eight months and twelve days, to be precise. And for nearly seven months he'd known there wouldn't be just one but two children. One clear and crisp morning in October, the gynaecologist had told his wife, 'You're pregnant with twins.' Looking at the monitor, the postman had seen two little curled-up creatures, in black and white, sleeping peacefully.

He couldn't believe his eyes. 'Two,' he whispered. 'Two.' For several minutes, two was an inconceivable number.

That night, the postman had rested his head on his wife's belly. 'Sweethearts,' he'd whispered through her navel. 'You two are our little sweethearts.' So from that day on, they referred to the peaceful, curled-up creatures in their mother's womb as 'sweethearts'. A room was decorated for them, socks were knitted, and the mothers-in-law were told they'd be getting sweethearts for grandchildren. One of them was so thrilled she baked a chocolate-pear-and-walnut tart that she proceeded to eat all by herself. And for the first time in a long while, she forgot she was eating on her own.

'I'll come and get you,' the postman said to his wife, and impulsively slipped the bag filled with letters, bank statements, and bills from his shoulder before hurling it over the wall that enclosed the garden of Number 5. He got into the small white *Poste Italiane* Fiat and raced home.

That day, many in the Rencio district of Bolzano waited in vain for the letterbox to rattle. Some people cursed the postal services; others cursed the entire country. And in hospital, the postman's wife cursed absolutely anyone she could think of. With sweat beading her nose and forehead, her eyes squeezed tight, and a string of ear-splitting expletives, she endured the worst pain of her life.

Giselle was the first to arrive. Small, red, and slippery, she squealed and flailed her arms about, as if to trumpet her arrival. Then came Fabrizio: likewise small, red, and slippery, but dead quiet and motionless. It wasn't until the midwife slapped and pinched his hands and the soles of his feet that Fabrizio gave a sign of life.

He sighed.

Both babies were placed on their mother's belly. For the first time they felt the outside of the body in which they'd been bobbing around for so long. The postman looked at his children — at his son and daughter, his sweethearts. Then he looked at his wife, her face tear-stained and the corners of her mouth practically soaring. He felt a way he'd never felt before, a way he never thought he would: complete and content.

But that's a different story.

The letter arrived unscented. The resident of Number 5b folded his newspaper, got out of his chair, and made his way to the front door. He bent down and picked up the envelope from the wooden floor. His name was written on the front in rounded, feminine handwriting: *Ezio Ortolani*.

He used his little finger to rip open the envelope. No scent rose up from the jagged edge, no perfume reached his nose, no forgotten atoms urged him to press the paper to his face. The envelope merely contained a letter that commenced as follows:

Caro Ezio, forgive me for writing and for responding only now. I have written this letter dozens, perhaps even hundreds, of times, but I never managed to send it. The words you're now reading are old and frail. The ink may be clear, my handwriting unchanged, but the words come from very deep down. They were stuck in my breast and wouldn't pass my lips, and later, when they were finally on paper, I crossed them out, blotted them out completely. Time and again, I tried not to write. But the longing won through — the persistent thoughts of us.

This letter has taken a woman's lifetime to reach you. Please don't rip it up. Time is running out. The days have become precious. We're old, Ezio. I'm a grey woman with wrinkles the size of furrows. You're probably as slow as a snail, or maybe you need a magnifying glass to read this letter. But when I think of you, it's not an old man I see. I see someone aged twenty-two, twenty-three — a young man in the prime of his life. I see you, Ezio, with your strong arms wrapped around me.

Suddenly the smells came flooding in, as if a steaming plate of pasta had been placed in front of him. *Linguine al cartoccio*. Except it wasn't squid, shrimp, or mussels he smelled, nor tomato sauce with finely chopped parsley and garlic, their flavours brought out by the olive oil. Ezio smelled blossoms. He smelled laundered dresses in the open air. And then he caught the scent of her hair, her neck, and the skin around her navel. It was an intense perfume he inhaled, held, and allowed to swirl around his body. After drifting through his belly and heart, the atoms of blossoms and summer dresses ended up in the gullies of his memory. They triggered a hurried search for the images that went with the scent: for the hair and the neck, the skin and the navel. And gradually, an image formed of a barefoot girl, of a twenty-year-old *donna Pugliese*, of the irresistible Giovanna Berlucchi.

Her words continued:

> *You were young and you wanted to kiss me all day long. But I also remember your trembling hands. You were scared and you loved me. Dear Ezio, I'd like to know whether your fingers still yearn for my skin, whether your eyes would like to see me, whether you'd want to kiss me now.*
>
> *I want to be with you, lie next to you, hear you breathe. The seasons change, but the days are all alike — today smells of yesterday, and*

yesterday tastes like the day before, and the day before yesterday sounds like any other day. The only thing that sets them apart is the feeling: the longing that intensifies, that seems to be growing with every passing day. These are the old, frail words I've kept locked in my heart for so long: I love you.

We haven't seen each other for more than sixty years. I don't know whether I thought of you every day, but I do know that I missed you every day. Do you think of me and do you think of summer when you do? Or are you still angry? You wrote that you were afraid you'd be angry for the rest of your life. I'm sorry I can love you only now, Ezio. I'm so terribly sorry.

I'd like to ask you to forget all those years we didn't share. Let's turn back time — stop the clocks and reverse the wheels — back to your bright eyes and my glossy hair. And if we're strong enough, stronger than the destructive wheels of time, back to Lecce, to a Tuesday morning in October, 1945. Let the train that took you beyond the horizon depart in reverse, so instead of disappearing you appear, and instead of getting on you get off and come to me, rather than leave me forever.

It's spring in Lecce. My heart is beating like

that of a young girl running across endless fields.
Ezio, be angry no more — be strong. Come to me.

He pressed the letter against his face, the white paper against his flaccid cheeks. There she was: the twenty-year-old young woman with bare feet.

It was July, the year was 1945. It was a warm day. The air shimmered in the distance. Ezio and his younger brother had gone to the beach. They'd walked eight kilometres and now they were lying on the sand, watching the women in bathing costumes walk by. The war was over, there was no work, and the days were long. What else was there to do for an Italian man but watch women?

Every day, Ezio and his brother would walk from Lecce to San Cataldo, a walk that could be done in ninety minutes, but sometimes took twice as long depending on the heat and the people they met along the way. Today they'd been held up by friends, aunts, and elderly men with long stories to tell. It was past midday by the time the Ortolani brothers finally arrived in San Cataldo, and now they were lying on the warm sand, their stomachs rumbling, watching the women in bathing costumes as unobtrusively as possible.

Not that there was a lot to see. The bathing costumes were one-pieces and sometimes even covered the knees and shoulders. The exciting moments came when a woman bent over to straighten her towel or when she emerged from the sea and outran the waves on her way back to the beach. At such moments, you didn't need the fantasy of a dozen writers to feel a tingling in your belly. You only had to keep your eyes peeled. The rest of the day it was a question of daydreaming and letting your imagination run wild about bathing costumes of all sizes but only a single shape: the one-piece swimsuit.

It was July 1945 — three months after the liberation of Italy and twelve months before the invention of the bikini. French mechanical engineer Louis Réard had yet to inherit his mother's lingerie business. He had yet to read a magazine article about the cost-savings of the US military, to be astounded by their decision to introduce low-cut backs to the bathing costumes of women soldiers. And above all: Louis Réard had yet to have the extremely simple idea that a two-piece swimsuit would save a lot more textile.

And a small group of islands between Papua New Guinea and Hawaii had yet to be bombed. The handful of residents living on this atoll in the Pacific Ocean were told to pack their bags and abandon their huts. For two long years, the families lived on a small coral island where the trees yielded too little fruit and the fish were poisonous, so they were moved once again and accommodated in tents on a stretch of grass beside the airport of another atoll, only to be relocated to

Kili Island six months later. But here, too, people went hungry and thirsty and many of their children died, until they were allowed to return to Bikini in 1969 when the atoll was declared free from radioactivity. However, in 1978, levels of radiation were found to be dangerously high after all, and the residents were told to leave their possessions, huts, and islands behind once more and they were evacuated yet again.

But that, too, is a different story.

Ezio was nudged by his brother. Nudging was a signal that a woman would come running out of the sea or could burst out of her bathing costume any moment now, or so their wishful thinking went.

Ezio looked up and his bright eyes scanned the shoreline of the Adriatic Sea. And that's when he first saw her, although his eyes didn't actually realise what they were seeing. It was more than a minute before he uttered, 'I see a navel.'

His brother only got as far as, 'Me too.'

There, in the surf, stood Giovanna Berlucchi. Incomparable. Incredibly beautiful. She was barely twenty, with long dark hair she always wore down.

That morning, she'd stormed out of the house after an argument. There'd been much yelling and slamming of doors.

The Berlucchi family was made up of six women — a mother and five daughters — and a much put-upon father. Giovanna was the eldest daughter and had to share her clothes with two younger sisters. Weddings, christenings, and the First Communions of cousins weren't just days to look forward to, but also days preceded by screeching, scratching, and crying. The three sisters would all want to wear the same item of clothing: a blue flowery dress, a cotton skirt with big pleats and a high waist, the only silk blouse. The father wore the same clothes day in day out and didn't understand why his daughters kept fighting. But then, it wasn't uncommon for him to be baffled by his daughters at the best of times. Experience had made him none the wiser; experience had taught him to remain silent as the grave. On one occasion he'd even incurred the wrath of his daughters by saying, 'If you don't stop bickering now, *I'm* going to wear that skirt to the wedding!'

The girls had looked at one another and forgotten all about the nuptials, the skirt, the bickering. They homed in on their father. It wasn't his business. He wasn't a woman. He didn't know what he was talking about. Why didn't he crawl back under his rock?

So when one summer morning there was a fight over a bathing costume and doors were slammed, a week's worth of dust whirled around the parlour, and the next-door neighbour crossed herself, the father didn't get involved. He remained tight-lipped, didn't move a muscle, and never even blinked. He just thought quietly of the son he would have loved to have.

The bathing costume stretched between Giovanna and her younger sister Francesca like a sheet about to be neatly folded. Neither was prepared to let go. What followed was a tug of war. Giovanna took a step back, Francesca a bigger one. The bathing costume stretched and turned a lighter colour. Giovanna took another step back, and in turn Francesca yanked at the fabric with all her might. The bathing costume was now twice its original length, and had it been quiet the agonised cries of the fibres might have been audible. But it wasn't quiet. There's no such thing as quiet in a house with six women.

'Let go,' Giovanna shrieked.

'No,' Francesca screeched. 'You let go!'

Meanwhile the father thought of a young man, an imaginary son who'd help him repair the roof — a roof that always needed fixing, even in summer, which is when the swallows took up residence beneath the eaves.

That's when it happened: the stretchy fabric tore. It happened in a flash, like a whip crack. The sisters fell to the floor, each with a piece of the bathing costume in their hands. Giovanna held the top half, Francesca the rest of the synthetic material. For a while the two sat facing each other, their eyes ablaze. They swore, calling out *stronza* and *faccia da culo*. Again, doors slammed, dust whirled around the parlour, and the next-door neighbour crossed herself. But this time the front door slammed as well. Giovanna ran out with the ripped costume in her hands. She was going to the beach. Nobody could stop her, and nothing would get in her way.

Louis Réard cut fabric measuring a little over seventy square centimetres into four triangles, which he then tied together with two bits of string. Giovanna Berlucchi needed only two knots. Having put on the top and bottom parts of the bathing costume, she tied a knot at the top left and one at the bottom right.

Twelve months later, not a single model was willing to wear Louis Réard's two-piece at a fashion show. In the end, only a nude dancer was prepared to don the garment. On 5 July 1946, Micheline Bernardini modelled the first bikini at the Molitor swimming pool in Paris. The newspapers were damning, speaking of 'moral decay' and 'a disgrace for France'. But when Giovanna Berlucchi walked along the beach of San Cataldo in her two-piece bathing costume and the sea air caressed her navel, she cast a lifelong spell over Ezio Ortolani.

Ezio Ortolani was eighty-four years old and had worked as an apple picker for the best part of his life. He lived alone, and was the kind of man who went to the same bar for his espresso every day. He rarely talked — he preferred to sit back and listen in silence. His friends had either died or were no longer able to get out and about. There was no woman in his life. There never had been. That's why he was on his own; that's why he was living out his days in Bolzano, the town to which he'd moved sixty years ago.

He'd fled.

At the age of twenty-three, Ezio wanted to close a door behind him and forget all about the room beyond it. But its contents were bigger than the room itself and seeped past the hinges and spilled through the keyhole, were more than willing to be carried on the wind across the silvery green seas of olive trees and vast vineyards, were seduced by a swarm of bees, and travelled in comfort from Carpi to Mantua on the roof of a train. Then again, sometimes they got stuck for days among the walls of a schoolyard, where they made little children miss their mothers. When the wind picked up, the contents of the room were lifted up yet again, over the walls, rising higher and higher into the sky, above the whooping of the children, over the houses, the trees, and the birds, before eventually raining down on an apple Ezio reached for with his right hand.

Having travelled the length and breadth of Italy, he'd finally ended up in a town where two groups of people were diametrically opposed to one another: Italians versus South Tyroleans. The war may have been over, but here another battle raged on — and had done so for nearly three decades.

Shortly after World War I, South Tyrol had been annexed by Italy. Without so much as a by-your-leave, practically overnight, as if it was perfectly natural. For the population of South Tyrol, however, it was anything but: from now on they had to speak Italian, their children had to attend Italian schools, and their surnames had to be changed to Italian names.

On the eve of World War II, people briefly entertained the hope that Mussolini might hand over South Tyrol to Hitler. But the two parties decided otherwise. And once this second war was over, too, and the borders were redrawn and reinstated, none was drawn between Italy and the annexed part of Austria. It was taken for granted that South Tyrol was part of Italy, although the vast majority of the people never did nor would ever feel Italian.

The battle in South Tyrol reminded Ezio of his own battle in Lecce. He'd done everything in his power to win over the beautiful Giovanna. But it hadn't been enough. Love can't be forced. And what's true for love, Ezio thought to himself, is true for culture.

He decided to withdraw and never go into battle again.

He became an apple picker.

The last variety to be harvested is the Morgenduft. Ezio had arrived in Bolzano in the nick of time to pick the red-and-green apple with the white freckles. On his first day in the new town, he'd gone for a walk along the Adige. He'd seen extensive orchards. Most of the trees were without fruit, but some bore large, gleaming apples. He couldn't help himself and entered one of the orchards. He was a man in the desert and this was the oasis he'd been seeking.

Ezio wanted to pick an apple, but a farmer wearing a blue apron stopped him from doing so. He went and stood in front of the tree as if it was the most important thing in his life: his wife, his child.

'I'd like an apple, if you don't mind,' Ezio said in Italian. He used a conditional clause.

'You guys want everything,' the farmer replied in the only Italian he knew: accusatory.

Ezio was tired. He'd been on the road for three weeks. He didn't want an argument. Nor did he want to leave, to flee again. 'I'm worn out,' is what he wanted to say. 'I'm hungry and thirsty and my heart aches. All I want is an apple.' But he couldn't get the words out.

The farmer stayed in front of the tree. Anyone wanting to pick his apples had to get past him first.

Ezio's eyes filled with tears. He'd travelled the length and breadth of Italy to leave the overflowing room behind, to make a fresh start. But now, here, more than a thousand kilometres from Lecce, he'd run into a man who wouldn't let him have an apple.

The farmer and Ezio continued to face off. But unlike the Berlucchi sisters when they fought over their bathing costume, the two men didn't say a word. They stared at each other in silence, their eyes blazing with hatred and misunderstanding. And if they'd had more eyes, those would have been filled with sadness and regret. But whatever a man feels deep inside rarely rises to the surface.

And then an apple fell from the tree behind the farmer. It was a round, almost entirely red apple, which had ripened in a good spot: high up in the tree, facing the sun, at the very tip of a branch. The piece of fruit, its skin as opaque as a glass frosted from cold, had been in the process of leaving the tree since early morning. Gravity had been tugging at the branch to which it was attached. The apple swayed in the wind, caught some rays of sun, sucked a final drop of moisture from the tree, and then the stalk broke f r e e from the tree.

It fell

    and fell

       and fell

          and was cushioned by an unsuspecting dandelion.

Next, the apple rolled a little way across the land before coming to a halt between Ezio and the farmer.

They looked down, their gaze followed by their inner eyes. This is what the farmer saw: the autumn of 1935; machines and men with axes and saws; fifty thousand fruit trees being cut down to make way for Italian industry. Stumps, branches, and apples everywhere he looked — hundreds of thousands of apples. It was autumn, and the harvest hadn't been brought in yet. He asked his father what was going on. But his father said nothing. His father said nothing for weeks, not even when all the wood and apples had been cleared away. Offices, warehouses, and workshops replaced the apple orchards. Homes were built for the workers. But this is what the farmer saw, and this is what his inner eyes kept seeing: a battlefield of fallen trees and apples.

Ezio didn't understand the film that was being played inside himself. The picture was blurred. It had something to do with time, and with an intimation of melancholy. For a split second he saw Giovanna on her doorstep. Her skin was bronzed, her freckled shoulders looked as though they wanted to be covered in kisses, and the tip of her nose was shiny.

Then Ezio picked up the apple and handed it to the farmer. Ezio may have fled, but he was no thief.

The farmer said something in German. He couldn't say it in Italian.

On the train, Ezio had learned two unpronounceable words: *Guten Tag*. That's as far as his knowledge of the farmer's language went. So he replied in Italian.

Both burst out laughing. In the end, the farmer used gestures to tell Ezio to come with him to the farm. There Ezio was handed an apron.

Later that same day, Ezio found himself picking apples with six other men in blue aprons. The following days, too, he climbed ladders, reached for apples that were as cold as ice, and gathered them in large wooden crates until the last fruits of the season had all been picked and the yellow leaves on the trees began to turn an orangey-red before taking on the brown hue of the earth on which they'd be falling.

The mornings turned colder. Polar lights were visible. The farmer's brother arrived from Petersberg, a village higher up in the mountains. He drove back and forth with steaming cow dung. Ezio and the other men spent a week shovelling shit under the apple trees. His skin was red with frost, his back a river of sweat. Ezio worked and shovelled, day-dreamed and reflected, but there were also times when he just listened to the landscape, leaning on his shovel, motionless as a rock — until a warning from the farmer drowned out the soft, ambient sounds.

By now, Ezio knew a few German words. Sometimes he even used one himself. He might utter a very solemn *Mahlzeit*, for instance. It would make his co-workers laugh, and Ezio himself laugh even harder.

Although his heart was still bleeding, he no longer felt the pain all day long.

Then the brown leaves started falling. They landed on the manure and together formed a fertile layer. The snow that came whirling down from the sky three days later covered it all in a thick blanket. Underneath, the fermenting compost slowly seeped into the soil, where it would ultimately feed and fortify the trees.

Winter had come.

Never before had Ezio felt as cold as he did during that winter in South Tyrol. Whenever he could, he'd sit in front of the fire. The farmer sent him to his brother's farm in Petersberg, where there were cows and Ezio could work without feeling cold. A cowshed is never cold.

So this is how Ezio spent the winter: milking cows and warming himself on the large animals. He relished the calm, the isolation. And after a while he no longer minded the pungent odour of the dung. He got used to the smell that clung to his clothes, his hair, his skin, his bed — to everything. In turn, the cows grew used to the man who'd sometimes hug them for minutes at a time.

Once the frost only materialised under the cloak of night and Ezio began to venture out of the cowshed more and more often, the time had come to return to Bolzano.

Ezio learned to take care of the apple trees. He staked heavy branches and thinned the crown so the light could penetrate the centre of the trees. He was initiated in the art of pruning.

'*Gleichgewicht*,' the blue-aproned farmer said. 'That's what it's all about.'

Ezio nodded without really understanding the word. He'd taught himself to nod whenever there was something he didn't get. If he let on that he didn't understand, a far more difficult explanation was likely to follow.

The farmer continued. 'Too much pruning harms the tree, which then yields just a small volume of large apples. But prune too little and all the energy goes to the tree itself and you end up with lots of small fruit.'

Ezio let the stream of words wash over him.

'*Gleichgewicht*,' the farmer repeated, as if it were something sacred, before climbing into an apple tree and showing him how to prune. Ezio then climbed the neighbouring tree and pruned it.

'*Naturtalent*,' the farmer said. And again, Ezio nodded without understanding the word. It was only after relieving dozens of apple trees of their branches that he realised what the farmer meant. He had a natural sense for the balance of trees. He, Ezio Ortolani, had the gift of seeing and feeling which branches should or should not be removed. It was as if he recognised something of himself in the trees, as if the branches were an extension of the arms that had held Giovanna. He knew how much there was to lose.

Later, the air became as sweet and delicate as butterfly wings. The buds of the pruned trees produced flowers. The blossoms were either completely white, or pink with white stripes. And the warm, high wind filled everybody with restlessness.

'Our work is done,' the farmer said to Ezio. 'Now we pass the baton to the bees and the wind.'

Nothing happened for days, except that the blossoms closed at night and opened again in the morning. But one day, the sweet air was charged with the buzzing of bees flying from tree to tree and from flower to flower.

Ezio leaned his back against a trunk and listened to the sounds of the land. He discovered that some apple pollen travels three kilometres on a bee's lower abdomen before pollinating the pistil of the blossom of a different species.

'Sometimes the wind will carry pollen across dozens of kilometres,' the farmer explained.

Ezio knew all about the wind's exceptional carrying capacity. The contents of the overflowing room in Lecce had managed to reach him all the way in Bolzano. The longing made its way through his entire body, making him feel as if the sun illuminated his soul. His imagination ran away with his memories. In his dreams, he secretly kissed Giovanna behind a tree.

Once the bees had done their job and the flowers in the apple orchard had all been pollinated, the sweet air rose up in slow, syrupy wingbeats. Shortly afterwards, the blossoms fell to the ground and the scent of spring was gone.

Summer was imminent: the light became warmer, the air heavier. Apples began to form on the branches. Ezio studied the various colours that appeared, disappeared, and stayed — yellow, green, pink, and red.

Finally, the August day arrived when the first apple of the season was ready to be harvested: the bright ruby Summer Red. The trees were picked over three times: first the sun-facing side, a week later the shaded one, and then after four more days the shadow side again.

The Summer Red was followed by the Gravenstein. Then came the Red Delicious, Idared, Winesap, and Granny Smith. And finally the Morgenduft again.

Ezio picked from August until November; he picked the first and the last apples of the season.

Summer and autumn.

Year after year after year.

Even during the years when South Tyrol was plagued by attacks — on army barracks, on overhead lines, on statues. These were the years when Sicilians were recruited to become *carabinieri* in Bolzano; the years when the battle flared up and culminated in the Feuernacht of 11 to 12 June 1961. During that night of fire, bombs destroyed thirty-seven electricity pylons and brought Northern Italy's industry to a partial standstill.

Interrogations, assaults, and murders followed.

Throughout those years, Ezio Ortolani picked apples, warmed himself on cows, and tended trees until the apples were ripe and ready to be harvested. He let the conflict pass him by.

But when the summer rains came and the river of time burst its banks, the distant memories rose to the surface again. On winter mornings, too, when Ezio sat on a milking stool and drifted away on the warm scent of milk, his mind wandered to the woman whose heart he'd been unable to conquer.

One conflict remained — not the one between two people, but the one within a single person: regret. And although his eyesight had deteriorated over the years, his inner eyes began to see the film that was played inside him more and more sharply. And that film felt like a stabbing pain.

Ezio Ortolani had stopped picking apples years ago. Even apple pickers retire. Now he was waiting for death, for Charon's boat, which had already ferried off his friends. But instead of death, a letter had arrived.

Ezio reread the bottom half. It was as though he couldn't understand the text, as though the meaning of the words eluded him. 'I love you,' he muttered to himself. 'I love you.' He got out of his chair and, with the letter in his hand, walked to the window, to the hallway, to the kitchen, all the while whispering, 'I love you.' Then, finally, the realisation hit home: Giovanna Berlucchi loved him. Giovanna, the girl who'd enchanted him with her navel and pierced his heart with the harpoon of first love. It had taken sixty years — the big middle section of his life, a slice before, and a considerable part thereafter — but now she'd answered the question that his mind had turned into the big riddle of his life.

As a boy, he'd felt unable to stay in Lecce; he'd felt compelled to flee, further and further north. As a young man, he'd thought there was no way back. It had nothing to do with pride. Ezio was inexperienced, unaware there was a way back. Now, nearly a lifetime later, he knew there was a way, but he'd come to believe in the irreversibility of things.

Some evenings Ezio thought that Giovanna had been ferried away as well, that unbeknown to him she'd made the crossing. He mourned her death, but it was the same sadness that washed over him when he thought of her bare feet and tanned shoulders. Was this the fate he'd inadvertently assigned to her? Whether she was young or in her eighties, whether she was dead or not, hadn't she always been a ghost drifting through his memories, in the underworld of his imagination? He'd failed to act. Like a lazy, old Orpheus he'd sat in his chair, staring into the dark night while hearing Giovanna's voice call out his name.

There'd been one moment when he could have turned back, one second of mercy in which he could have looked over his shoulder without losing her.

'Please stay,' Giovanna had said. Her eyes were red. They were standing face to face at Lecce station. He wanted to wipe away her tears, wrap his arms around her. But instead he made his way to the train, unable to stay.

'Ezio,' she said.

He stepped onto the footboard of his carriage.

She yelled his name with tears spilling into her mouth. 'Ezio! Ezio!'

Little did he know — only Giovanna knew, and even she only half-knew, because the full understanding, the sense of loss, the never-ending longing, came much later — that all he had to do was turn around. She'd have come running and she'd have flung her arms around him. The whistle would have sounded, but it wouldn't have haunted her memories. Instead, Ezio boarded the train and Giovanna walked out of the station, destined to hear that shrill signal every silent day of her life.

Ezio, the old, the lonely, folded the letter. His hands, the hands that had picked thousands of apples and extracted thousands of litres of milk, were trembling. Had it all been for nothing — the flight, the isolation, the life among the trees and the cows? His hands were shaking just as they used to when he held hers. He'd hoped that one day he'd be as hard as steel, but he still felt the arrow in his chest.

There had been a time when she wasn't uppermost on his mind. He was in his fifties then; he had friends, and he wasn't unhappy. He spent his weekends hiking in the Dolomites, while in summer he climbed their three-thousand-metre peaks. The views, with the Alps in the distance, were awe-inspiring. He signed his name in the registers beside the big summit crosses: *Ezio Ortolani*, followed by the date and sometimes even an exclamation. *Grande*! He was often the last of his group to leave, lingering by the cross, taking in his surroundings: the bare tree tops, the mighty depths, the silence. None of his friends knew about Giovanna. He'd never mentioned her to anyone. They saw him eat, drink, and be merry in huts sporting the German names of flowers. He wasn't unhappy, yet he was far from complete.

His heart had started bleeding on the train, a loud steam train spewing out smoke and soot. It had been a dark day in October. The sun had gone into hiding, the people were quiet. Ezio looked out of the carriage window, past his own reflection. He saw vast, bare fields, alternating with the locomotive's smoke. And he saw Giovanna's red eyes and he heard her cries. He smelled her skin, felt her hands, and tasted the sea on her lips.

His journey ended up lasting three weeks. He was eager to leave Lecce behind — behind the horizon and in memory — but the noisy train he'd boarded went no further than Foggia.

Taken aback, Ezio got off and followed the other passengers along the platform. On the station concourse, he tried to get information about train times. A man in a dark-green uniform pointed to a board, in front of which a bunch of old men had gathered.

Ezio made his way there and overheard the gripes of the people around him. 'I can't read those letters,' someone said. 'They're too small.' Another man complained, 'I can't see them at all.' When Ezio finally got close enough, he read that the next northbound train was due to depart in two days' time.

'Please stay,' he heard Giovanna's voice say.

But he walked away without looking over his shoulder. Feeling restless, he left the tiny station of Foggia. He was hungry, weary, and cold. In summer, he could have slept in the open air — under a pomegranate tree or under the starry sky. Instead, Ezio roamed the streets of Foggia, in search of a warm place where he could put his feet up. His eyes scrutinised the houses, seeing the occasional light or shadowy shape behind the windows.

One of those shadowy shapes was Signora Rinaldi, the mother of a soldier who hadn't made it back from the war. When she saw Ezio walking down the street, a loud shriek escaped her lips. She ran outside and hugged the half-frozen young man. She cried, and because of the tears failed to see that she was showering a complete stranger with her love. Ezio was too tired, too weak, and too sad to resist the fat arms that squeezed him tight and the wet mouth that kissed him. Before he knew it, he was sitting in the kitchen with a plate of pasta in front of him.

'Eat,' Signora Rinaldi said. 'Eat, my child.'

And eat he did. Ezio ate like a prodigal son. He devoured two plates of pasta and a hunk of stewed meat.

Signora Rinaldi had become a shadow of her former self. The words *Matteo didn't make it back* had robbed her eyes of their glint. Since those words, she spent every day waiting for her son's voice, staring out of the window for hours on end and, after dark, pressing his pillow to her chest like a baby. Even now that her tears had dried, she couldn't see it was Ezio who was eating the reheated osso buco. She saw the son who'd finally come home: Matteo Rinaldi, barely twenty, with his whole life ahead of him. He'd joined the army happily enough. He'd seen conscription as an opportunity, as a chance to escape everything familiar and boring. As a boy he'd dreamed of the ocean liners setting off for America, but it was an experience he'd never have. If Matteo hadn't fallen — a bomb dropped by a US B-17 on 16 August 1943 — he'd have had a career in the army. Years later, he'd have been stationed in South Tyrol as a colonel. He wouldn't have met Ezio Ortolani, though. As an apple picker, Ezio lived a long way from the attacks and the clashes between terrorists and army. Fate would never have brought them closer than this.

That night, Signora Rinaldi didn't get out of bed. Nor did she walk to the front door to see if her son might be standing behind it.

When, after two days, Ezio said *I have to go*, Signora Rinaldi walked with him to the station. Her feet darted across the paving stones, and on the platform she didn't say *please stay*. She said goodbye — at long last, she was able to say goodbye to her son. And by the time the train was no more than a dot on the horizon, her eyes were gleaming.

And so Ezio travelled northbound. He got off in Pescara, where he was offered a lift by a milkman. While walking to Tortoreto, he was allowed to hop on a farmer's cart. And in San Benedetto del Tronto, Ezio took the train to the next city and moved further and further from the south.

Nights were spent in the houses of people he met on the road. Sometimes he didn't even have to ask for a place to sleep. The farmer who'd given him a lift had also offered him bed and board. Perhaps people saw the sadness in him. After a week on the move, he'd acquired big bags under his eyes. His dreams, in unfamiliar, hard beds, were frequented by Giovanna, who whispered in his ear, caressed him, and kissed him on the forehead. But as soon as Ezio tried to embrace her, his hands would be grappling with sheets and he found himself kissing the cold bedroom air.

It was on the train to Faenza that he first uttered her name. Having fallen asleep, he ended up caressing the seat's upholstery, while his lips were puckering up for a kiss. 'Giovanna,' he whispered. 'Giovanna.'

'No,' he heard a voice say. 'Bruno. My name is Bruno.'

Ezio opened his eyes and looked at the man sitting beside him.

'*Tua fidanzata*?' Bruno asked.

Ezio shook his head. Giovanna wasn't his fiancée. And this thought upset him so much he doubled up in pain.

'Is everything all right?' Bruno asked in a deep voice, and put a hand on the young man's shoulder. 'Is the train going too fast for you?'

Ezio shook his head. It was his heart, he wanted to say, but he couldn't utter a word.

'Keep breathing,' Bruno advised. 'My wife always feels nauseous on the train, too.'

'I don't feel nauseous,' Ezio uttered with the greatest difficulty.

'Do you have a headache?'

Ezio was now bent double, with his forehead resting on his knees.

'We're nearly there,' Bruno said, and began to massage Ezio's shoulder. 'Faenza isn't much further.'

Faenza was only twenty minutes away, but Ezio couldn't bear the spasms in his chest a second longer. He wanted to rip out his heart and hurl it out of the compartment window.

Some boys become men by sleeping with a woman, others by shooting a deer or crashing a car. And then there are boys who become men on a train, bent over with a hand on their shoulder. Ezio felt Bruno massaging him gently, but it didn't help. It was this thought that made him a man: *I'm all alone in the world.*

Ezio woke with a jolt. The letter fell to the floor. He felt his heart pounding in his chest. He was on medication, but didn't always take it in the prescribed doses. A year more or less, what did it matter? The days were all alike. In autumn he put on a heavy coat, mid-spring he took it off again.

After he retired, when he couldn't head up into the mountains anymore and his friends were dying one by one, he began to feel regret. Ezio looked back on his life as a match he'd lost. His younger self was to blame. So now, as an old man, he was stuck, forced to hear every solitary second of time tick away. While others might go on a cruise to Cape Horn or spend the winter hibernating in the Caribbean, Ezio stayed in Bolzano. He listened to the days passing by and eventually reached the conclusion that he'd never met anyone he loved as much as he'd loved Giovanna.

Ezio had met other women. Most were no longer girls and read books and liked to cook for him. He'd had a brief relationship with a forty-year-old teacher who'd been abandoned by her husband. It didn't amount to much — a mere echo of love. Her children might be the same age as his, if he'd had any.

The thought that it had all been in vain could leave Ezio feeling furious, although he never really knew whether to be angry with himself or Giovanna. He imagined her life had simply carried on and that her heart had no qualms about other men at all.

He often wondered what might have become of him had he stayed in Lecce. He wouldn't have picked apples. Maybe he'd have gone to work for his uncle, eventually taking over the fishmonger's in the harbour. Would it have made any difference?

Ezio stared into the middle distance, trying to picture the grey woman with wrinkles like furrows, but her young girl's face wouldn't be disfigured by age. Her arms remained slender, her breasts round and firm. In his memory, it was always summer. He could still smell her, and the thought of her mouth conjured up the taste of salt.

Ezio was afraid her lips might crack if he kissed her now.

The long-gone day when the Ortolani brothers lay on San Cataldo beach and Giovanna walked into the surf in a two-piece bathing costume often rained down on the apples Ezio picked.

Giovanna had been aware of the two young men staring at her, but pretended not to notice. The twenty-year-old *donna Pugliese* had plunged into the sea, diving down to reach a shell on the bottom. Giovanna could hold her breath longer than three of her sisters combined. She had the lungs of a dolphin. As a child, she'd alarmed her parents on numerous occasions by staying under water long after all the other children had resurfaced. Ezio and his brother weren't alarmed, though. Mesmerised, they gazed at the water that had swallowed up the woman with the navel, thinking they'd witnessed a Fata Morgana. This was the price to pay for prolonged staring at bathing costumes, and the fantasies that went with it: a woman who dissolved in the sea.

But then Giovanna emerged from a wave, her long hair falling in strands over her shoulders. Seawater flowed down her smooth belly, gushing over the small hollow of her navel. She was even more beautiful than before.

The two brothers froze in the sun. The wheels of

time seemed to falter and the gears grind to a halt. Only Giovanna kept moving. It was just a split second, but long enough for an everlasting lead. Ezio knew he had to do something before his brother did.

Suddenly Ezio leapt to his feet and started running. He ran over to Giovanna. His strides were big and his knees strong; his heart was pounding and his cheeks were red. The blood surged through his veins and his lungs filled with air. But there were no words in the speech centre in his brain. He ran and ran and ran. And then he stood before her, before the goddess from the waves with the gushing navel. He panted and looked at her eyes. Eventually, a thought formed in Ezio's mind. *They're chestnut-coloured*, he thought to himself. *Her eyes are chestnut brown.* He looked at them and lost his heart.

'*Ciao*,' Giovanna said, in her hands the shell she'd just brought to the surface.

Ezio's gaze travelled from her eyes to the shell and from the ribbed pink shell back to her reddish-brown eyes.

That's when the questions came — a barrage of them. *What have I done? What am I doing here? Why did I start running? Where's my brother? What am I supposed to say?* But no answers were forthcoming.

The waterfall around Giovanna's navel had all but run dry. What remained was a glistening residue of salt.

Finally Ezio said: 'Now that I'm here, do you mind if I kiss you?'

It was pure swagger, as suggested by the slight quiver in his voice. Ezio had never asked a woman *Do you mind if I kiss you?* Not even in his dreams.

Giovanna laughed. Perhaps he could have known then, during those few seconds when Giovanna was laughing, that she'd never love him the way he loved her: unconditionally and solemnly, as if it was a matter of life and death.

The connection between love and laughter mustn't be underestimated, but a light-hearted laugh isn't the same as one seeking to requite love. Perhaps it's the exact opposite: a laugh seeking to sidestep love, to keep it at a distance, far from the heart.

Still, she nodded. Giovanna Berlucchi nodded and closed her eyes. She waited, clutching the shell and wondering where the young man with the bright eyes would kiss her: on her right or left cheek? On her forehead? Gallantly on the back of her hand? Boldly on her lips? When she didn't feel anything after five seconds, she puckered up her lips. She'd decided that he should kiss her on the mouth. But Ezio was gone. Just as he'd run to Giovanna, he'd walked away from her — with great haste and a racing heart.

Ezio plonked down in the sand beside his brother.

There was a brief silence.

Then came the question: 'What did you do?'

'I don't know.'

Meanwhile, Giovanna had opened her eyes and was staring at the empty space in front of her, momentarily stunned. Then a vicious expletive escaped her unpuckered lips. She stomped over to Ezio. Her feet left deep imprints in the sand, her elbows jabbed the air, and her wet hair resembled the tentacles of an octopus. Only her navel seemed oblivious to her fury. Like a sun, it shone in the open sky of her naked belly.

The first thing she said to Ezio was, 'You've got three seconds to kiss me. Or I'll scream.'

Ezio sought help in his brother's eyes, but those seemed to be rolling in disbelief.

'One.'

'I'm sorry,' Ezio whispered.

'Two.'

He tried to find bigger words. Soothing words. Words capable of calming a woman. But he had no idea what to say. Ezio came from a family of men. He had no experience whatsoever with sisters or female cousins.

'Two-and-a-half.'

He had to act. Ezio had to act really fast now. He got up, but only halfway, and ended up on his knees. It occurred to him that his body and will were out of sync. But it was too late. His mouth approached her warm skin. He kissed her navel.

This might have been the story — the story Ezio and Giovanna told their children, and their children's children, too. The story that would bind them together forever. *The* story.

But this is a different story.

Two things happened that day.

Ezio and his brother fell out. For the first time, they didn't walk the eight kilometres back to Lecce together.

'Try to understand,' Ezio pleaded. 'Please, try to understand.'

But his brother didn't understand. He felt betrayed and walked home alone. And with every stone he kicked aside, he cursed 'the whore with the navel'. The Ortolani brothers didn't speak for the rest of the summer, and when one grey morning in October they bumped into each other in the living room and Ezio told him he had to go, his brother didn't stop him. He didn't try to talk him out of it. They were afraid to look at each other, but their inner eyes saw a definitive farewell.

After Ezio had kissed Giovanna's navel — a place that hadn't crossed her mind, sending a shiver through her belly that unfurled its wings and began to flutter — they walked to the sea together. They sat down in the surf with their feet in the water and their toes in the wet sand.

They sat without speaking and stared at the horizon.

Nothing happened. They felt the warmth that infused the sand and the shells, and this warmth was all they wanted. Yet Ezio had the peculiar sensation that his body was about to erupt, as if its contents were fermenting, its molecules moving faster and faster. Something inside him was trying to find a way out. He felt a hot surge of energy rush from his belly up through his chest, where it collided with a bone that was too hard to crack. The energy was propelled to Ezio's neck and squeezed through his windpipe, up to his larynx. Here, the surge was converted into rapid vibrations that bounced every which way inside his mouth. Finally, it burst open.

He asked her to marry him.

Giovanna didn't answer. She placed the shell she'd brought to the surface against Ezio's left ear. She let him hear the sea.

But Ezio was solemn, even then, and he repeated his question.

Giovanna was different. She loved being alone; her heart was fearless and undaunted. Maybe she was ahead of her time, the way her swimming costume was ahead of its time. She didn't think she could ever love just one man. She wanted to be free.

She rose to her feet and waded in up to her waist. Maybe she only loved the sea, in which she could remain submerged for so long — longer than anyone else.

She plunged in.

Ezio watched the ripples left by Giovanna and felt a resinous gloom take hold of his body. And unlike the surge of energy that had caught him unawares moments earlier, this gloom didn't try to find a way out. It would sink deeper and deeper and would eventually take root in his body.

Under the water, Giovanna waited for Ezio. She knew he'd come looking for her. Her father used to dive in after her, too. It was a game. He was aware that she had the lungs of a dolphin and wasn't drowning, yet he'd always jump in and lift her out of the sea. Giovanna was older now, no longer a child, but that didn't stop her from playing the game.

Ezio ran into the water and dived down to where he'd last seen Giovanna. When he spotted her, he grabbed hold of her waist and swam back to the surface. It flashed through his mind that, having saved her life, she had no choice but to marry him. But before she'd even taken her first breath, Giovanna had already burst out laughing. The sadness, which tried to move down a level in Ezio's body, could be halted just in time. Because this, too, happened that day: Giovanna pressed her bubbly, laughing mouth on Ezio's, and their lips came together.

He keyed in the phone number at the bottom of the letter, underneath her name. It took a while before he heard a female voice. He didn't recognise it, as it seemed suffused with a rustling sound. The woman spoke softly, yet her words possessed the same strength as those Giovanna had spoken to him as a girl. He was delighted to finally hear her again. The last time he'd heard her voice had been at Lecce station.

'I'm coming to see you,' Ezio said.

Some sort of shiver went through him, one of joy rather than fear. It felt as if he was on his way to her already, as if he'd always been on his way to her: in the apple orchard, in the Petersberg cowshed, in his small apartment in Rencio. Even while he was moving away from her on the train, he'd actually been on his way to her.

Now, at long last, he was going to arrive. The young man who'd left would return as a grey old man. He'd been on a journey, an odyssey, much like the scientist who'd ventured into the jungle for research and ended up living among chimpanzees for more than twenty years.

Giovanna asked him to tell her a little bit about himself.

Not knowing where to start, Ezio began by saying he didn't have children. She listened to his voice, which had grown deeper and which faltered occasionally, as if some of the words had to get used to the space they were suddenly granted.

Ezio fell silent.

He didn't want to have a conversation over the phone, not after sixty years. In the evening, he'd pack a suitcase with a shirt and trousers, a pair of socks, and underpants. He'd go to bed early — he always went to bed early — and the following morning he'd walk to the station and board the train to Lecce. Her address was on the back of the ripped-open white envelope. It was a street he'd passed through countless times as a boy. He remembered a bakery and the smell of almond croissants. Ezio would take a taxi to her house and press the doorbell. Then the door would open slowly and they'd talk and find out everything there was to know about the long lives they'd lived so far apart.

But Giovanna began to cry. He heard her sob. And so he said, 'It's okay. I'm not angry.' He took a deep breath. And because he didn't know what else to say, he repeated, 'I'm coming to see you.' He felt tears of his own well up. He wanted to hold her hands in his, and he wanted it so badly he almost cried. But he fought back his tears. He'd always fought back his tears.

Giovanna asked him when he'd be coming.

'Tomorrow,' Ezio replied. 'I'm leaving in the morning.'

He knew there was a daily train to Lecce. The Intercity covered the 1,082 kilometres in thirteen hours and four minutes, stopping at thirty-seven stations along the way. Ezio had often seen the train depart from Platform 6.

But he never got around to boarding. *That's the way back*, he used to think to himself. *That's the way back to Giovanna: more than a thousand kilometres southbound, setting off in daylight and arriving after nightfall.*

'I'll be waiting for you,' Giovanna said, sounding as if she'd always been waiting for him, as if he'd made frequent appearances in her dreams and she'd whispered his name.

Neither of them spoke. The murmur of the sea could be heard down the line. They briefly saw the same vision, as both of them drew from the well of their past, and they were sitting there again, in the surf, under the San Cataldo summer sun.

Then Ezio said, 'See you tomorrow,' and carefully returned the receiver to its cradle.

The following morning, he left his house with a small suitcase in his right hand. It was early; there was still time for an espresso in his local café.

The barista looked at his suitcase. 'Is everything all right, sir?' he asked when he put the cup down in front of Ezio.

Ezio remembered drinking the father's espresso. The son used the same beans. In all those years, the flavour hadn't changed, the aroma was still equally strong. It's possible that something intangible remains unchanged over decades, while everything else changes.

Ezio nodded to the barista and took a sip.

Soon after, he walked over to the station. Although he wasn't as slow as a snail, as Giovanna had suggested, he did take a little longer over things these days. That said, there was no rush; there was no harvest to be brought in.

His train was listed on the departure board in the concourse. Ezio went to the ticket desk. There the lady serving him repeated his destination. 'Lecce,' she said. 'Are you sure?'

Had he lost his mind? Is that what was happening? It wasn't too late. He could stay, he could go back home and unpack his suitcase.

Ezio had never seen his mother again. She'd died, and so had his father, and perhaps his brother, too. He'd written his family only once. It had been a short letter. In it he apologised, asking them to forgive him his flight. He didn't ask for their understanding. He'd also written something about apple trees dropping some of their fruit in June so they don't collapse under their own weight.

The woman at the desk looked at him.

Ezio nodded. He was sure. 'Second class, please,' he said. 'A window seat.'

The Intercity was ready on Platform 6. Through the loudspeakers came a monotonous rundown of the stations along the way: 'Ora, Mezzocorona, Trento, Rovereto, Verona Porta Nuova, Mantova, Carpi …' Ezio looked over to the green mountains. He'd never thought the region would come to feel familiar to him. Farms high up in the mountains, cable cars, snow in winter — shortly after his arrival in Bolzano he'd regarded it all with astonishment. Was this Italy? The differences between the South Tyroleans and the Italians remained, but nowadays they couldn't exist without one another. Young people were bilingual.

Ezio boarded the carriage indicated on his ticket. The train was made up of old-fashioned cars with a continuous passage and individual compartments. He lifted his suitcase into the luggage rack above his seat and sat down. He looked out of the window, at the people on the platform, at the farewell rituals. Then the whistle sounded and the train jolted into motion. No other passengers had joined him in his compartment.

At first Ezio saw vast apple orchards. The trees were younger and smaller than they used to be, and planted closer together. Special tractors had been developed that could be driven up and down the narrow paths. Next up were the vineyards. Since spring was warm this year, the harvest would be early, yielding glorious, heavenly bunches. Then the train began its descent, leaving the mountains behind. Ezio regarded the landscape he'd travelled through all those years ago by steam train, on foot, in a farmer's cart. Finally, he was taking a proper look back.

In Rovereto, an older lady entered his compartment. Not once, not even when the train went through the tunnels outside Verona, did she take off her sunglasses. Ezio couldn't tell whether she was looking at him or not. Every now and then, he allowed his eyes to rest on her body. She was wearing black — a loose-fitting skirt suit. Her hair had been dyed, and the pale roots showed. Ezio wondered if she might be a warning. He hadn't been this close, for this long, to a woman in years. The nylon material of her tights revealed twisted veins. His memories had better prepare for the worst.

When the lady got ready to leave the compartment just before Bologna, Ezio heaved a quiet sigh of relief. He'd scrutinised every centimetre of her appearance, down to the age spots on her neck.

The train waited at Bologna station for nearly half an hour. When the whistle finally sounded, the other seats in his compartment remained empty. Ezio was looking forward to the rest of his journey. He'd bought two newspapers at a kiosk, and then of course there was the landscape flashing by like a film being rewound.

That's when the door slid open. The first thing he saw was a plume of dark-brown hair. A girl's voice spoke to him, curtly: '*Buongiorno.*'

Ezio was too stunned to return the greeting.

She sat down beside the window and took a look at the old man opposite her.

Ezio glanced away, at the station sliding past. An optical illusion. The train had got going again — he was the one moving, making the long journey back.

When the train was at full speed, he plucked up the courage to turn his head and look at the girl opposite him. She'd closed her eyes. Her face was red, her skin flushed. Her chest was moving up and down. She must have dashed across the station concourse, up the stairs, and down the platform, to catch the departing train.

Ezio ran his eyes over her body, over the t-shirt that revealed a hint of her bare stomach, over the skirt that ended halfway down her thighs, the skin red from running. This, too, was an optical illusion: her body billowing towards him. He could feel the warmth emanating from her skin; it enveloped him. Ezio was aware of her breathing, the billowing of her body. He seemed to be swaying, swooning, and then he let the waves wash over him.

Her warm belly was right in front of his mouth, so close his nose touched her skin. He kissed her navel and said in surprise, 'I smell blossoms.'

'My turn,' Giovanna exclaimed, and pushed Ezio onto his back. She was taller and stronger than he was.

After their first kiss, Ezio had wanted to carry Giovanna out of the sea, but she kept slipping from his arms. His clumsiness made her laugh.

Now, several warm nights and long days later, they were back on the beach, frolicking in the languorous sunshine.

Ezio had gone over to her house. He'd stood in front of the Berlucchi family home for a full five minutes before he summoned the courage to knock on the front door. A girl with honey-toned skin answered. Ezio introduced himself and asked for her sister. The girl stared at him and then yelled as loudly as her small body allowed, 'Mama! Mama!'

Giovanna's mother appeared in the doorway. Her body was large and her forehead wide but smooth. She wasn't all that old yet. Her bushy eyebrows were dark blonde.

Ezio introduced himself again and explained that he'd come for her daughter.

'Which one?' the mother asked. 'I've got five.'

He wanted to say that he'd come for the daughter with the breathtaking bathing costume, the daughter he'd kissed and wanted to marry, but he only managed a very soft 'Giovanna'.

The little girl had her mother's voice, he realised, when she shouted Giovanna's name. Three protracted syllables, then the last culminating in a crescendo.

Ezio could see all of her teeth.

When her sister didn't appear straight away, the little girl asked her mother, 'Why does he want to see Giovanna?'

'Why don't you ask him?'

Ezio could feel himself blushing. He tried to find words to distract her — words that might placate a little girl. But again, he had no idea what to say. Too many men in his family.

Giovanna came out, taken aback by the sight of Ezio. Taken aback, but amused, too.

Instead of leaving them in peace, Giovanna's mother and little sister hung around and were joined by the other three Berlucchi women. The only one who kept a low profile was the father. He was praying for the young man's life.

Ezio's breath caught in his throat.

Then the little sister asked, 'What do you want?'

Ezio looked at Giovanna, but she didn't come to the rescue.

Her mother and sisters burst out laughing. The whole situation was beginning to feel like a scene from an opera.

Eventually, Ezio asked if Giovanna wanted to go to the beach.

Against a backdrop of hysterical laughter from the chorus, the eldest sister said 'yes'. Finally and unexpectedly: the first yes.

An hour and fifteen minutes later, they arrived in San Cataldo. They'd covered the eight kilometres in record time by chasing each other, and when they caught sight of the sea they removed their sandals and ran barefoot onto the beach.

Ezio waded into the water in his underpants. Giovanna put on the ripped bathing costume right there on the sand, plunged into the sea, and vanished.

What followed was the same old game: when Giovanna didn't resurface, Ezio went looking for her, found her, and brought her back up.

'Kiss me,' Giovanna said. 'Go on then, kiss me!'

Ezio closed his eyes and leaned in, but Giovanna had already slipped from his arms and disappeared under the water. He dived in after her and tried to bring her back to the surface, but she refused to be recaptured. Again and again, she managed to escape from his arms. She was like a dolphin, and relished the game.

Back on the beach, they panted with exertion. They plonked down on the white sand, lying side by side in the sunshine. Ezio wasn't sure if Giovanna wanted him to kiss her. And so minutes passed; minutes that felt like days, which in turn felt like weeks, months, years. Silence lasts an eternity when there's a girl lying beside you.

After seven hundred years, Giovanna said, 'You can rest your head on my stomach, if you like.'

Indeed, it felt as if an eternity had passed when, after

seven hundred years, Ezio finally got to touch Giovanna's stomach again. He kissed her navel.

'I smell blossoms,' he said in wonder.

'My turn,' Giovanna exclaimed, and less than two seconds later she was lying on top of Ezio and pressed her mouth to his navel.

Giovanna smelled something other than blossoms. She smelled something she couldn't immediately place. Maybe the closest thing was the opposite of blossoms: an odour reminiscent of death and decay.

'There's something inside your navel,' she said. 'And it needs to come out.'

'What is it?' Ezio asked.

'It stinks.'

Giovanna got up and ran away. Ezio was too stunned for words. He stayed where he was, closed his eyes, and prayed for a deluge to sweep his body away. He was afraid she wouldn't come back, that the stench was unbearable. Would he ever be able to hang out with girls, be easygoing around them, without always fearing the worst?

'I found something!' Giovanna yelled.

Ezio opened his eyes to see her towering over his stomach with a smile.

'What are you going to do?' Ezio asked.

'I'm going to remove that thing from your navel.'

'What thing?'

'That dark thing,' Giovanna said, 'that's really smelly.'

He felt something enter his navel — the tip of a small twig or a stick.

'It's stuck,' Giovanna said. 'But not for much longer.'

'It hurts.'

'Shh.'

Ezio tried to put a brave face on it, but when he felt as if she was rummaging around in his navel with the tip of a knife, he squealed.

'Relax,' Giovanna said. 'It's out.'

She dangled a twig in front of his eyes. On the end was a moist and murky little pellet.

'What is it?' Ezio asked.

Giovanna shrugged her shoulders. 'A mussel, maybe?'

What he saw when he looked at the dark thing was the abyss of love. Ezio was terrified she'd get up and abandon him there on the beach once and for all.

'Do you still like me?' he asked.

Giovanna was absolutely fascinated by the mussel. 'Shall we put him back in the sea?' she suggested.

Ezio nodded, afraid to repeat his question.

Giovanna rose to her feet and hurled the branch with the grubby little pellet into the water. Then she leaned back over Ezio — her face over his stomach, her mouth close to his navel, smiling, kissing, and teasing him.

Ezio felt Giovanna's lips touch first his navel, then his lower belly, the edge of his underpants, and for a split second the fabric that rose millimetre by millimetre.

Giovanna's eyes were ablaze. 'Your turn now,' she said. 'Kiss me.'

Ezio looked around. A couple lay sunbathing less than a hundred metres away. The woman's eyes were closed, the man had a newspaper in his hands.

'Are you scared?' Giovanna asked, laughing just as her sisters and mother had done.

It was one of those moments that would later rise like a luminous vision from the mists of his memory. The image of her face, her mischievous laugh, even the ambient sounds — everything would come back. And then Ezio would want to kiss her again. Again and again and again.

Giovanna shifted onto her side, one elbow in the sand, resting her head on her hand. Her body was a wave.

He kissed her navel, he kissed her lower belly, and he kissed the knot of the bathing costume that used to be a one-piece. He brushed his lips across the tightly stretched, narrowing fabric, and when he didn't know what to do next, Giovanna moved her hips. She was kissing him with her body.

When they were lying side by side again, they didn't speak. They watched the sky and felt as if they were floating.

At dusk, when the horizon turned crimson and the water black, Ezio escorted Giovanna home. He held her hand for eight kilometres.

The spluttering from the loudspeakers sounded like applause at the opera. Those who weren't tourists and had a good pair of ears knew the next stop was Pescara. The sea was visible behind the windows along the aisle: rippled and ultra-marine.

The young lady opposite Ezio had gotten to her feet. She'd failed to notice that her skirt had ridden up. Ezio wanted to look away, but something inside him was stronger. His gaze was drawn to her thighs: the young skin, its warm tint, its sheen. He looked at them the way he'd looked at the images in his mind for all those years. Yet now it felt like a farewell to this beauty. The skirt wasn't pulled back in place; it simply slipped down again — slowly, irrevocably, like a curtain falling.

'*Ciao*,' the young lady said.

Their eyes met briefly. Then she slid open the door and walked into the aisle. Ezio caught one final glimpse of her, with the sea in the background. Then she was gone.

The operation, the removal of the mussel from Ezio's navel, hadn't gone without a hitch. There were complications. It began with a bit of irritation, but soon after Ezio started feeling nauseous. And in the days that followed he suffered terrible stomach-aches. He drank a cup of olive oil and went to the toilet every hour. Ezio blamed the pain on his bowels, on some dodgy food perhaps. It never occurred to him that it could be something else. Finally, the doctor told him he had an infection in his navel.

'Strange,' the doctor said, removing pus with a cotton bud. 'A strange place for an infection.'

Ezio didn't tell him that someone had been poking around in it with a twig and extracted a grubby little pellet. It wouldn't have made it any less strange.

He left the doctor's house with a tube of ointment, bent double, because he was in too much pain to walk straight. And so Ezio learned that the person you love can also hurt you. But the longing wouldn't actually admit this thought. He yearned for Giovanna, for her smooth belly illuminated by the sun.

After the navel inspection, he saw her three times. And each time they strayed further from the sea, enjoyed longer kisses, and floated a little higher. But then the pain became unbearable. Ezio wondered if he might be afflicted by desire, by the lust that wanted to gnaw through the elastic material of Giovanna's bathing costume. Perhaps he was.

After his visit to the doctor, Ezio spent three days in bed. Then he could walk upright again. And it was upright he made his way to Giovanna's house and knocked on the front door.

The washing was drying in the sun. On the line, among the dresses flapping about, were underpants.

The biggest were white, the smallest pink. Ezio inhaled the scent of lavender so deeply that some of the atoms lingered in the conduits of his memory.

Giovanna opened the door. She smiled, but never once during the entire walk to San Cataldo did she say she'd missed Ezio.

He'd missed her terribly. During each bite, each step, each heartbeat, and each breath, he'd whispered her name, while his belly felt close to bursting. The combination, the mix of navel pain and longing, was too much for one person to bear.

Giovanna was happy to be outside and darted down the road to San Cataldo like a sparrow. Ezio's hands were trembling, including the one holding Giovanna's. He held her tight, worried she might fly off, float away without him.

Within hearing distance of the sea, in the lee of a small sand dune, his fears were stilled. Mind you, not immediately. First, there was silence: one hundred, two hundred, three hundred years. Again, Ezio didn't have the courage to kiss her. Why, oh why was he so scared? What should he be scared of? Ezio heard the voice of reason addressing him, but what does reason know of trembling hands and a heart pounding like that of a hunted animal? Nothing. Sure, later, with hindsight, it can make sense of it all, muttering and musing like an old man.

Seven hundred years.

'Kiss me,' Giovanna whispered. 'Kiss me all over.'

He drew closer, kissing her navel and lower belly, and with each touch that followed, his mind grew quieter and his desire greater. When his mouth reached the bottom of her bathing costume, his desire was greater than ever. Greater than himself. The lust gnawed through the bathing costume.

'Use your fingers,' she whispered hurriedly.

He used his fingers, his trembling fingers. Everything was new, and everything was soft — so soft it made him dizzy. It was the same feeling you get when you light a cigarette after a long time. Giovanna smiled in a way he'd never seen her smile before: vulnerably. That first time, Ezio had kissed her navel unintentionally, but this time his actions matched up to his will. He used his mouth and tasted of the forbidden fruit.

Giovanna's lower body jerked. She moaned and groaned and floated.

Before Ezio knew it, he was lying on his back and felt Giovanna's mouth on his navel, the navel that hadn't completely healed yet. She kissed him gently and caressed him with her tongue.

Giovanna's desire, too, broke through the fibres separating him from her.

Ezio felt her hand, which, unlike his, was strong and firm. He shuddered at her touch, and then it all happened very fast. The first time it always happens very fast.

Afterwards, while watching the big sky above the sea with Giovanna's head on his chest, Ezio felt that warm glow surging through his body again. But this time, he kept the words in their prison and stopped them from breaking free.

They breathed as one and savoured the day that passed and would only return in their dreams.

Ezio didn't want the day to end, though. He didn't want to dream. He wanted to do it all over again: knock on the front door, inhale the scent of freshly laundered dresses, walk to San Cataldo, float in the sand pit. In a word, everything! And so he reappeared on Giovanna's doorstep the following day. There was no washing on the line, but that was a mere detail.

Giovanna opened the door. She kissed and hugged Ezio, and was happy to be whisked away. They retraced the steps taken twenty-four hours earlier, left the same footprints on the beach and, in the lee of the small sand dune, relived the previous day.

Again, some things were different: lips explored a neck, a hand touched a breast. Plus: it lasted longer. Not much, just a little.

And so the summer passed: the days grew shorter, the pleasure lasted longer. Each time, Ezio managed to delay the climax further. But the more he managed to contain this passion, the harder it became to contain that other glow inside.

In October, when even the Southern Italian summer had come to an end, Ezio asked Giovanna to marry him for the second time.

They'd spent the entire afternoon in the sand pit. The sun sank into the immeasurable sea, shells closed, a container ship disappeared beyond the horizon. Ezio and Giovanna watched the breaking waves and let the murmur wash over them.

They'd walked to the water's edge, Giovanna's left hand in Ezio's right. It felt clammy and trembled a little. He tried to suppress the shaking by clenching his teeth, but it only seemed to make his hand twitchier. His fingers felt like live wires. The hot surge of energy that had erupted from his belly and had tried to find a way out through his chest had ricocheted to his shoulder and was now trying to exit via his right hand.

The energy shook Ezio's hand out of Giovanna's and pulled him down, down to the beach. The soft, wet sand welcomed his trembling index finger. Without fully realising what he was doing, Ezio wrote out a question. The letters were all over the place, but there was no mistaking the message: *Will you marry me?*

As Giovanna looked at the spidery letters, she seemed to sense a danger. First she took a step back, her eyes still on the question. Then she looked up, but instead of meeting Ezio's gaze, she walked into the water.

It was late October and the sea was really too cold for swimming, but that didn't stop Giovanna Berlucchi from diving in and disappearing under the water. Ezio remained behind with his message, which was erased by three waves.

Following his departure from Lecce, she'd returned many more times to the shelter of the small sand dune. But never alone. Giovanna wanted to be free, without obligations, without commitments. Somewhere inside, she sensed an emptiness after Ezio's departure — a void that wouldn't be filled, that would never be filled. But that realisation came only later, after dozens of years. The first time Giovanna returned to the sand dune, she felt liberated.

Wanting to make the most of the last bit of warmth of the year, she made almost daily trips to San Cataldo beach, which was now bathed in soft, reddish-yellow light. This is where she seduced young men, caressed their navels, and broke their hearts. But whichever boy Giovanna kissed, the following day she'd have forgotten all about him.

A year later, by the time Ezio was picking green apples with red flushes in Bolzano, she'd caused more heartache than her four sisters combined ever would. But it wasn't the same pain that Ezio had felt. It wasn't a harpoon that couldn't be yanked free. The boys Giovanna forgot, they forgot her, too. The odd one burst into tears and stamped his feet, but eventually he gave up as well. Other men got over it after a year and the loss of five kilos in body weight. They ended up marrying the daughter of a net-maker or an olive farmer — caring women who gave them children with thick, dark hair.

None of them fled.

By then, the bikini had been modelled by a nude dancer in a glitzy swimming pool in Paris. The Vatican deemed the garment immoral and banned women from wearing it on beaches. But Southern Italy lives by different rules than the rest of the country. And so it happened that Giovanna could wear her two-piece bathing costume during the long summers and enchant countless men, who'd stare at her as if they were seeing a mirage. She didn't fall in love. Never. It could be seen as a form of protest — against a bourgeois mentality or against the natural course of things — but the truth was that Giovanna was incapable of giving her heart to anyone else. However fast she walked the road to San Cataldo, however high she floated, her heart was hers and hers alone. The only thing she always longed for was the sea, in which she'd remain submerged for as long as possible.

By the time Giovanna reached her mid-twenties, she still hadn't opted for a different life. She didn't want a husband and children. Would she ever? Her mother was worried and tried to talk sense into her. 'Marriage isn't a prison,' she told her daughter. 'Children aren't chains.'

Giovanna said she was happy and didn't need anyone. 'I don't believe in marriage.'

Her mother's eyes filled with tears. 'Later,' she said. 'Later, you'll see what I mean. When you're old and the people around you start dropping away one by one.'

Giovanna said she had no interest in later. 'I live in the present!' she exclaimed. Her voice was louder than she intended. Her father, who was in another room, heard her and knew what was coming.

Giovanna's mother raised her voice, too, accusing her daughter of being stubborn and selfish.

Halfway through the blazing row that followed — once again, doors were slammed, dust whirled up, and the woman next door crossed herself — Giovanna ran away from home. For three years she lived with a man she didn't love, and only left him when he raised the prospect of children, of a daughter with the same honey-toned skin as her, the same glorious navel, and the same bare feet. With a suitcase in her hand, Giovanna ran to the station in Lecce. She made her way down the same platform as Ezio had years earlier, and the train she boarded was headed in the same direction, too. But

Giovanna travelled no more than two hours. She got off in Ostuni, the white city by the sea. This is where she found a job as a chamber maid and slept in the only room without a view of the Adriatic Sea. This is where, for the first time, she cried about her life and the pain she was inflicting on others.

For three months, she didn't smile at a single soul.

For six months — the time between the harvesting of the apples and the flowering of the trees — she didn't touch a single man.

But by the time the bees in Northern Italy were covering dozens of kilometres with pollen on their backs, and the air smelled sweet, like soft red fruit, Giovanna was walking along the beach, warming herself in the sun and letting the sea breeze caress her navel. An older man with grey eyes and dark brows fell for her charms. He invited Giovanna to dinner in the old town. Drunk on Negroamaro, she ended up in his hotel room. Drunk, she touched him everywhere. Drunk, her lips moved all over his body. But she was sober when the man burst into tears and told her about his wife and three children in Brindisi. Giovanna grew quiet and looked at the man's damp cheeks. She'd seen plenty of tears in her life, but never those of a man with a wife and three children.

'I'm sorry,' the man muttered. 'I'm sorry I want it and that I'm lusting after someone other than my wife.' He pressed his head into Giovanna's lap. She let him and stroked his hair, listening to the muffled snivelling and the occasional, inarticulate lament. Then the man began to lick her, like a young animal, a playful dog.

'I want it,' Giovanna heard him say. 'I want it again.'

It made her laugh, laugh uncontrollably, and she fell backwards onto the bed, shaking her head. But the man wouldn't be put off by Giovanna's glee. He kissed, caressed, and licked her. And that's when it happened: Giovanna grew quieter until her laughter died down altogether. She was floating over the sand dunes and the sea.

Back in the dark hotel room, in the clammy bed, Giovanna stared at the man. He was afraid to return her gaze.

'Now what?' Giovanna asked. She smiled. And because the man didn't reply, she said: 'We can carry on seeing each other, but you mustn't fall in love with me.' She wanted to remain in control. She'd make sure nothing went wrong this time around.

The man looked at Giovanna. Seeing her beauty, he felt a warm glow inside. But he also saw her bold smile. Feeling apprehensive, he was briefly tempted to get up and go back to his wife and three children. But beauty conquers all.

Giovanna jotted down the phone number of the guesthouse where she worked. 'Say you're my brother,' she instructed him.

The man nodded and learned the number off by heart on his way back to Brindisi.

Nine days later, the woman running the guesthouse called Giovanna over: a phone call from her brother.

And so she became a mistress — not a wife, not a mother, but a woman who meets a married man in secret places at odd hours: in a car park in the middle of the night, out in the open in a field while the farmers are away for lunch.

But the man with the grey eyes and the dark brows fell in love, too. It happened very gradually — bit by bit, day by day. Once the love made itself known, there was no denying it. Over dinner, the man told her that he wanted to leave his wife and children, and marry her.

Giovanna didn't touch her food. 'It's over,' she said, put down her napkin, and walked out of the restaurant.

There were many more phone calls from the brother, but each time the guesthouse owner could only tell him the same thing: his sister was gone and would probably not be back. Giovanna had disappeared overnight.

Then there was a Hungarian man Giovanna lived with in Budapest in the late 1950s. She'd followed him — not out of love, but because she wanted to get out of the heel of Italy, where most days were warm and dull. Maybe she wanted to feel the cold, the real cold that never reached Apulia. The Hungarian was happy enough for her to tag along. Like Giovanna, he was independent and non-conformist. He travelled around Europe with two suitcases filled with horse leather, deer skin, and wolf pelts. His hands were as rough as fig leaves. And this man, of all men, was the one who got her pregnant. She was scared, unbelievably scared, but pleased as well. She'd always thought she'd feel alienated from her body if she ever got pregnant, that she'd grow to hate the embryo in her womb, but instead she caught herself touching her belly and gently caressing the skin with her fingertips. Even though she'd never wanted children, with each day that passed Giovanna felt happier and more complete.

When she was eight weeks late, she told the man who smelled of wolves that she was pregnant. He flew into a rage, yelled, and smashed up a table. Giovanna was scared he'd hit her with his rough hands — he had a look in his eyes. She fled the house and sought refuge in a coffee house, where she warmed herself on the small cups. When she came home late that night and tried to sneak in, the front door wouldn't open. She shouted the name of the father of her unborn child through the letterbox, but he refused to open the door for her.

He didn't want her, just as she'd never wanted a man, a man who'd cling to her, who'd claim an ever greater piece of her life.

And so she went back, back to Lecce. Throughout the train journey — three nights and two days — she kept her hands on her belly, holding the unborn child so as not to lose herself. If Giovanna had disembarked in Bolzano, she could have breathed out the same little clouds as Ezio in the apple orchard. But she had no way of knowing where he was, and her thoughts hadn't drifted back to him yet.

Giovanna knocked on the door of her parents' house, and when her mother opened up Giovanna's eyes filled with tears. Another door that remained shut would have been unbearable.

The mother took her child in her arms and rocked her back and forth. At the kitchen table, Giovanna was served a big plate of pasta. 'Eat, my child,' her mother said, which is what all mothers in Italy say to prodigal sons and daughters.

Giovanna's mother didn't ask any questions. Food is more important than words. Besides, she knew. She could tell from her daughter's face, from her mouth. Not only did Giovanna eat the pasta, but she also devoured the leftover pieces of *torta pasticciotto* her mother had made that afternoon.

Giovanna found a job in a pizzeria. She worked six days a week, from noon till night, carrying carafes and glasses, plates and cutlery. And the embryo in her belly bobbed around with every step. After closing time, she often spent another hour at the bar with the pizzeria owner and his children, who helped wait tables. Giovanna was the only one who didn't drink. She held her belly instead.

During a busy lunchtime session, she suddenly got cramps. She ran to the toilet, where she took off her apron and pulled down her skirt and underwear in one fluid motion. Drops slid down her legs; big, viscous drops, like tears made of jelly. At the sight of blood, she clapped her hand over her mouth. The next moment she had to hold on to the wall.

Giovanna went home at once. She opened the door and walked straight past her mother. In bed, she lost even more blood. She screamed and cried, and for the first time in her life she felt abandoned.

But the massive wheels of time didn't stand still. They moved on, steadily and invisibly, ticking off the seconds, grinding up the days, weeks, and months as though they were grain.

And then, suddenly, fifteen years had passed — fifteen summers since Ezio's departure from Lecce.

Giovanna still worked in the same pizzeria, but had started sneaking away at mealtimes. She'd walk the road to San Cataldo and then she'd sit on the beach. The wind went in search of her navel, but it was buried under two layers of fabric. She rummaged in the sand, hiding her hands from herself, afraid to touch her belly.

Every day, she'd stare a little longer at the water that merged with the sky in the distance.

In South Tyrol, meanwhile, the highest peaks were covered in snow; the mornings were cold, the apple trees still in bud. There was no horizon to be seen.

One day Giovanna walked into the sea, fully clothed. She didn't dive. The waves washed over her face, her head disappeared. She stayed under for a minute, two minutes. If her father had been standing at the water's edge, he'd have dived in after her. But there was nobody at the water's edge: neither her father, nor Ezio. Giovanna gasped for breath in the sea, and for a moment or two it looked as if she'd finally lost the game. But then she came up spluttering and somehow managed to reach the shore. Back on the beach, she vomited water.

She walked the eight kilometres back to Lecce, looking bedraggled. People who saw her go by stared. But the men who'd once kissed her lips averted their gaze. Her clothes were dripping wet, her ankles caked with sand. She was oblivious to the sun casting its glow over her.

At home, in bed, Giovanna tried to still her cold, shaking hands. She swallowed and pressed her hands to her stomach, crying all the while. And so she sat for an hour. Her belly grew warmer and gradually got used to her hands. But there was one place she hadn't touched yet. She shivered, afraid to look. Gently, Giovanna felt her navel. Her fingertips tingled at the touch. The next moment she felt a tremor, a shiver running through her entire body. It came from very far, that shiver, and so did his name.

Memory may be unreliable and selective, but it's not incoherent. It makes connections: between scents and fields, between sounds and an old square in the centre of town, between caresses and people. The tender, transparent antennae of Giovanna's memory remembered a kiss, a mouth, a man.

For the first time in a long, long while, she thought back to the summer of 1945; to the four months that had passed in the romantic blur of youth; to the young man with the bright eyes. To Ezio Ortolani.

The following day, Giovanna didn't go to work. Instead, she headed straight to San Cataldo. She found the hollow in which they'd lain and where desire had gnawed through the fabric of their clothes. She strolled to the spot on the beach where she thought Ezio had traced words in the sand with his index finger, and pictured the spidery letters, merely a step and fifteen years away. She wondered what her life might have been like had she said yes. She couldn't help it — it was her imagination: standing beside her on the beach was a young girl with honey-toned skin and the same bare feet as herself.

Giovanna tried to find out where Ezio lived, and whether he was married or still a bachelor. Whether or not he had children. But nobody could give her any answers. Rumour had it that Ezio's parents blamed Giovanna for their son's departure, so she was afraid to contact the Ortolani family.

Then the longing came.

The longing that grows steadily when it isn't satisfied, and grows stronger when the questions remain; the longing that finally sprang up from the deep well of the past.

At some point in the Sixties — the bikini had arrived on Europe's beaches, and Ursula Andress had emerged out of the Caribbean Sea in a white version and become immortal — Ezio's mother fell ill. She developed a pain in her breast, which then spread to the rest of her body. It was terminal.

Giovanna saw the placard with the death announcement on the wall beside the bakery. The funeral would be in three days' time.

She'd go with her face veiled so nobody would recognise her. She didn't want to ruin the ceremony.

It was well-attended, as all funerals are in the south. There were relatives and neighbours, familiar faces all around. Giovanna spotted Ezio's brother beside the grave. He still had thick dark hair, and a relatively unlined face. Only his back was a little bent. Alberto Ortolani worked in the harbour, where he sat outside on a bucket every morning, cleaning freshly caught sea urchins. He was never seen without a cigarette dangling from his lips.

Following his brother's departure, at the end of the last summer of his youth, Alberto had gone to work in his uncle's fishmonger's. It was a small shop, and at first he was less of a help than a hindrance, if truth be told. But that's the order of things: you help your family, smoke cigarettes, and eventually take over the business. And this, too, was part of it: Alberto Ortolani got married and had three children, all sons. At the funeral they were standing behind him, next to his wife, a woman who'd never been outside Apulia and had never known the longing to get away. There was only one kind of soil: the kind on which you grew up, on which you had children, and in which you were buried.

Ezio had to be a few years older than his brother. Giovanna tried to picture him in his forties, a middle-aged man with crow's-feet, but with the same bright eyes he had on San Cataldo beach.

Years passed; many, many years. Giovanna's dark hair lost its lustre, her wrinkles deepened. Every now and then she'd meet a man, but those encounters brought little joy. She never floated these days. It seemed as if every kiss was pointless and every man made her feel more alone. Giovanna's mother had given up hope. She'd resigned herself to the fact that one of her daughters would never be married. But even though she had nothing to complain about with fourteen grandchildren, she still screamed for joy when one afternoon in November a letter for her daughter arrived. She recognised the name on the back of the envelope: *Ezio Ortolani*.

Giovanna thought her mother was talking gibberish — she was old and prone to muddling things up. Occasionally, she'd address the doctor by her husband's name. Her memory made connections that either didn't exist, or existed only in her wildest dreams.

It was a letter overflowing with emotion. Ezio had finally written to Giovanna, because he'd lost the fight not to write. He'd been fighting for forty years. *This letter is as old as the years that have passed,* he wrote. *I still feel the same — the same anger and the same yearning, the same hope and the same despair. The bottom of my memory is littered with letters, with questions, with lonely mutterings, and with big words.* And then she read the big words that had survived nearly half a century of turmoil: *Write me everything, or write me nothing at all. Say you love me.*

Ezio and Giovanna wouldn't have survived another

forty years of silence. But Giovanna's letters also floundered, one after the other. She wrote back right away, a long letter about the life she'd lived without him, but the big words were missing. She'd never told any man she loved him. In fact, she didn't even know if she could love someone. Sure, she felt lonely. Sure, she'd begun to long for Ezio. And sure, she wanted to see him. But was that enough? Giovanna was afraid she'd end up hurting Ezio even more. *So maybe it's better if I remain alone*, she ended her letter. *But then again, maybe not.* As well as long, the letter was confused. Luckily, it ended up in the bin. Love is complicated enough in and of itself.

Giovanna's mother died a few months later. On her deathbed she advised her daughter: 'Marry on a summer's day and you'll never feel old.' Her sisters all thought their mother had well and truly lost her mind. And maybe she had, or maybe, in a moment of clarity, she remembered Ezio's name and thought back to the summer when she and her daughters had laughed at the diffident young man who'd courted Giovanna.

Giovanna wrote a second letter. She covered both sides of a piece of paper, but this time the sentences were shorter and her words clearer. She folded the sheet in two and put it in an envelope. She wrote Ezio's name and address on the front in her round handwriting, stuck a stamp on, and left the letter on the sideboard, ready for posting.

The following morning, Giovanna strolled to the letterbox and lifted the letter to the slot, but then realised that it didn't contain the big words. She withdrew her hand and slipped the letter into her coat pocket. Back home, the envelope was put on the kitchen counter, only to be moved to the top of the fridge soon afterwards. But here, too, it was in the way and so it ended up in the fireplace, where the flames feasted on the clear words and short sentences.

In the years that followed, Giovanna didn't write any letters, because she simply couldn't get 'everything' said. She couldn't even say the big words in her head. It felt as if they were and would always be abstract to her. Some women remain alone, and are perhaps destined to remain alone. No candles are lit on their graves, no tears are ever shed for them. Perhaps Giovanna Berlucchi was one of these women.

She didn't marry on a summer's day. She didn't marry at all. Giovanna grew old. Her hair turned a dirty yellow, her face became heavily lined. She sold her parents' house and moved into a smaller place in the old town centre, not far from the Chiesa di Santa Chiara. In the morning, the aroma of freshly baked bread wafted up to her living room.

While unpacking the boxes, she came across Ezio's letter. Giovanna spent an entire day re-reading his words, and an entire night thinking of the past. Some memories sent a stab of pain through her lower abdomen. That night, she gently lifted her gown and looked at her belly — the belly that didn't have room for love or a child. That's when she finally saw what she'd been feeling all these years: a scar that wouldn't heal, that would never heal. Giovanna placed her old hands on her stomach and caressed her navel.

She whispered his name as if she were talking in her sleep.

Another year passed before Giovanna wrote the letter she would eventually mail. There's not much to say about that year, except this: the days were all alike, whether or not it rained, flowers opened up, butterflies dried their wings, or waves shimmered in the setting sun.

She capitulated, wrote down the big words, and sent the letter to Ezio. It disappeared in a hessian mail bag that was lifted onto a truck. Three hours later, the letter arrived in Bari, where it passed through unknown hands before disappearing once more in a dark bag. The journey continued by goods train with a destination of Verona. Here the letter swam in a gigantic school, through various basins, and ended up in a white plastic tray. On day one, the tray stayed where it was; on day two, it was transported; on day three, the letter arrived in the right place, where it was handled by the postman sorting the mail for the Rencio district. First thing that morning, he'd urged his wife to call him as soon as her contractions started. 'I'll come over at once,' he'd said.

The letter very nearly never arrived. The postman had pushed the white envelope through Ezio's letterbox and let go the moment his phone rang.

The letter fell

and fell

and fell

and the postman's wife announced the most beautiful day in his life.

The train arrived on Platform 4. Ezio lifted his suitcase out of the luggage rack and left the compartment in which he'd spent fourteen hours. The train was an hour late; the driver had smoked a cigarette at practically every station.

Giovanna stood halfway down the platform, next to the stairs leading up to the concourse. She was convinced she'd recognise Ezio, even from a distance, but she didn't want to take any chances. She'd been wondering how to greet him, what to say to him. But what do you say when you meet again after sixty years? What words can span such a huge distance? Those very same questions had been on Ezio's mind during the latter part of his journey, but he had no answers. He had that same indefinable feeling as all those years ago, when he'd run over to Giovanna with big strides and red cheeks — with great speed, but without words.

When Giovanna spotted two lights in the distance, her eyes filled with tears. The tracks had begun to hum, a humming that grew louder and louder, as if the sea was about to engulf the land. Giovanna held on to a bannister, her white hair bobbing in the air stream of the approaching train.

She spotted him immediately, the boy who was now an elderly man. Ezio cautiously disembarked from the train. Another passenger offered to help, but he declined. If he took it easy, he'd be fine.

That's when he saw her. The barefoot enchantress aged eighty. He saw her white hair and the wrinkles in her face. And he also saw the beauty that was nowhere to be seen.

Giovanna stood still, the way she'd stood still on the day of his departure. Both felt a twinge in their hearts. But the pain was short-lived. Ezio walked over to Giovanna, retracing his steps from sixty-two years ago. She looked at him, and let her tears run freely. Ezio wanted to run. He desperately wanted to put his suitcase down on the platform and run to her with strong knees.

The closer Ezio came, the better he saw her, yet Giovanna's outline never fully sharpened. This was the image he'd always been unable to picture. Everything had faded: her youth, her dewy skin, her voluptuous figure. But Ezio knew the years had wreaked just as much havoc on him; his eyes were no longer bright, and the two of them would never again cover the distance to San Cataldo in an hour and fifteen minutes.

He dropped his suitcase — the suitcase that contained no more than a shirt, a pair of trousers, underpants, and some socks. During the long journey he'd asked himself what would follow their reunion, what would happen next.

But by the time Ezio finally wrapped his arms around Giovanna, and she put her head in his neck, and they stood there like two entangled statues, the question had all but faded from his mind. It felt as if nothing would follow, as if this was the final station, the end.

No words came. There was only silence. Dead silence. One hundred, two hundred, three hundred years.

Four More Stories

The Ticket Inspector

This was to be his last spring. It was the warmest within living memory. Heinrich Kienzl could think of no finer one, and he had more than seventy years to fall back on. He remembered spring as a child: white blossoms and a stroll with his parents. He'd flown between them like an angel, tiny and light and happy.

It was early April and thirty degrees Celsius. Swallows whooshed through the air. Heinrich Kienzl had taken the cable car up to San Genesio to escape the heat. The mountain station was a thousand metres above sea level. During the ride he'd gazed at the meadows down below. The grass was green all over, with large clumps of dandelions scattered about. Other colours would follow later: the purple of clover, the blue of gentian, the white of milfoil.

For forty years, Heinrich Kienzl had hovered over

the meadows of San Genesio. He'd been a cable-car conductor. Inspecting tickets and operating the controls in the cabin had been an undemanding job. He'd spent most of the time looking out of the window, where he saw the chestnuts grow, the land being tilled by the farmers, deer fleeing back into the forest first thing in the morning, the last butterflies of the year.

The staff at San Genesio Cableway didn't know him. They were young, in their early thirties. The conductor who'd inspected his ticket was sitting on a stool, reading a graphic novel. The stool was new, but otherwise nothing had changed inside the cabin: the same controls, the same black phone hooked up to the mountain station. And the maximum number of passengers remained unchanged, too — twenty plus one, the conductor.

Heinrich Kienzl had joined the cable-car company as a twenty-year-old lad and had left it as a slow old man. His first and final working days bookended a life up in the air. It hadn't been a great adventure, nothing like that dream little boys have of wanting to touch the clouds. He'd been only a few metres above the ground, just a little higher than he'd once flown in between his parents.

Nine minutes: that's how long it took the cable car to glide from the valley terminal in Bozen to the mountain station in San Genesio. Bridging a height of 741 metres, the cable was nearly two-and-a-half kilometres long, and suspended from seven reinforced concrete pillars.

In his final year as a conductor, he'd tried to calculate how much of his life he'd spent gliding. But every night, smack-bang in the middle of a multiplication, Heinrich Kienzl would fall asleep.

Nobody had spent more hours in the cable car; nobody had seen more.

He'd seen Johanna Egger grow up. On Wednesday 19 August 1964, her mother wheeled a pram into the cable-car cabin, seven days after little Johanna's birth. She was his youngest-ever passenger, her downy face filled with wonder. During the descent, when the change in pressure made the baby cry, she was lifted from the pram by her mother and breastfed. By the time they reached the valley terminal, she'd fallen asleep.

In what seemed like the slowest of slow-motion, he saw Johanna grow into a girl who skipped through life, curious about everything. Some days she smelled of soap, on others as sweet as French toast. Then she grew tall and thin and withdrawn: a young woman hiding in baggy clothes. The shame she felt towards her body was all too apparent to him. But once that shame had been conquered, he saw a beauty coming out of her shell. Summer brought with it the soft skin of her arms, tanned legs, and feet in sandals. The sun worshipped her for twenty-five years: in the fields of flowers, on the shores of small mountain lakes, on a horse galloping across the sandy paths of Salten. Finally, Heinrich Kienzl saw the lines around her eyes, very fine ones, a mere hint of things to come. He wouldn't get to see the rest of the engraving.

Heinrich Kienzl didn't have children of his own. He'd never married. At the end of her life, his mother had asked him if he preferred men. He'd shaken his head. A wife — it just never happened.

It was one of those things: there were farmers without wives, too. They had land, they had livestock, but they had nobody beside them in bed. Perhaps they'd been hopelessly in love once upon a time. But let's hope not. Some farmers lived with their mother or an aunt, and she would do the washing, the cooking, and the sowing of spinach in the garden.

The butcher of San Genesio had never married, either.

Heinrich looked at the trees with their tender leaves, foliage so green it was almost luminous. He felt a real lust for life, just as in the old days, when his hair was still dark. He was grateful. Of course there was melancholy, too, and some hours were slow as treacle. He put it down to loneliness, the darkness in winter: memories he couldn't ward off, crossroads at which he'd found himself. The life that might have been if only … But he wasn't sad. No, Heinrich Kienzl wasn't unhappy. At night he watched the stars for hours on end.

The mountain station was just outside the village centre. Heinrich was the last of the string of people who'd taken the cable car up. Trailing behind, he noticed that the cows hadn't been let out yet. The grass had to grow some more. The new hay barns, built by the timber merchants at the foot of the village, were gigantic. The farmers would be fertilising the land just before the rains came. But when would they come, the rains? The Dolomites in the distance shared the sky with the sun.

In San Genesio it was warm, too, but unlike in the valley, there was a breeze. Heinrich made his way to the inn and sat down outside. The landlady recognised him at once. Frieda. She knew everything about everybody in the village.

'Long time no see,' she said.

That was true. The last time Heinrich had taken the cable car up had been in autumn. The first snow had followed two weeks later: ninety centimetres overnight.

He asked how things were going and whether the first guests had arrived yet. Frieda nodded curtly. She didn't like to talk about herself or the inn. She preferred to talk about others.

'White wine?' she asked.

No reply was needed. She knew what he liked to drink.

Heinrich looked at the gently rolling meadow in front of him. At the top stood a house where a couple lived. It was the most beautiful house in the village, or perhaps even the entire region. It stood with its back to San Genesio. In the morning the sun rose out front, above the mountains, and in summer the evening sun illuminated the rear of the house until late. There was a bench. The place tickled Heinrich's imagination, but it also left him with a tinge of sadness. There had been a crossroads long ago, and he'd taken the wrong path; an opportunity, and he'd missed it.

He drank his wine slowly. He had time, an awful lot of time. The mornings felt the longest. He began his day on a chair in the front room. From behind the large window, he watched everything that moved: the many men in their cars, mothers with children, housewives on their way to the butcher's, farmers on their spluttering tractors. Later, the street gradually emptied to finally come to a complete standstill around noon.

Suddenly Frieda appeared by his side. 'Luis was picked up in a helicopter yesterday,' she said. 'He ought to cut down on his smoking and drinking. This is his third time in hospital.'

Heinrich knew Luis, an electrician with tall tales. He used to take the cable car every day. And every year he packed on another kilo.

'Asthma,' Frieda said disapprovingly. 'And to think he lives as though he's invincible.'

'Do you think he'll pull through?'

'He always pulls through.'

Heinrich wondered how Johanna Egger was doing. Was she married? Did she still live in San Genesio? Frieda would know.

'That's the problem,' the landlady said. 'He never learns.'

Heinrich took a sip of wine. He'd seen a lot of men disappear. Walter Durnwalder had lost control of his car after one too many. Franz Laimer had collapsed during a hike. And only recently, his former colleague Stefano Calvo had died in his sleep.

Frieda looked at him.

'It's a beautiful spring,' Heinrich finally said.

When the sun's light began to mellow, he rose to his feet. He walked back to the cable car, past the rolling meadow, past the most beautiful house he'd ever laid eyes on. He saw a stooped man, and although he was far away, Heinrich could see him quite clearly. In the rich glow of the evening sun, the man was feeding animals in cages — rabbits who'd survived Christmas.

Maybe he hadn't missed any opportunities, he thought to himself while waiting for the cable car. Maybe there hadn't been any. He'd got to know quite a few people in the cabin of San Genesio Cableway, and with some he'd established a bond. He used to talk to them and listen to their stories — nine minutes one way in the morning, and nine minutes back at the end of the day. It wasn't much, but then again, how much time do married couples spend talking to each other?

It goes without saying that Heinrich had also spent time watching — feasting his eyes on women, that is. He liked a perfect face: youth, unadulterated beauty. There were some women he missed when they didn't take the cable car, women he'd been watching for years. But most of them were the mothers of young children. He also remembered a tourist from Germany. Her hair was blonde and her mouth delicate, with the lips of a princess. He'd seen her for fifty-four minutes of his life. It was a simple sum, but the rest would be forever shrouded in mystery. She was staying at the inn with a female friend. Heinrich looked into her eyes and she looked back. She kept looking.

It all happened very fast: the longing, the conversations in the cabin about walking trails and their lives, her hands touching his. 'We're travelling home today,' she'd said as she disembarked. His heart was beating twice as fast; he could feel it pounding, palpitating almost. Had this been the opportunity life had offered him? Had this girl been the woman with whom Heinrich Kienzl could have grown old?

The cable-car door opened and the first few passengers started boarding. Heinrich remained seated. There was time. In two, three minutes, a signal would sound, as the conductor down in the valley pressed the lower button on the control panel and gave the all-clear for departure.

Inside the cabin, people talked about the weather: the sun, the heat. A hiker had been high up in the mountains where he'd seen a sea of crocuses. His arms and nose were sunburnt. Heinrich looked at the meadows below him, which were as pretty as a travel-guide picture. Having seen it many times, he knew how green the grass would grow. The first few years, he'd been oblivious to the process. The world appeared to have turned a different colour overnight. In reality, though, it happened very, very gradually. It wasn't a wave, not a single broad movement. Some areas of land were less drab, scattered patches that grew lighter, that appeared to come to life, before slowly, day by day, weaving the carpet into an even surface until everything was deep green.

He knew what came next: the blush of dandelions sweeping across, followed by the other colours, the buzzing bees and the singing cicadas, and then, finally, the last butterflies of the year.

Down in the valley, it was five degrees warmer. Heinrich waited for the bus that would take him to the town centre. Across the road was a sawmill. On rainy days, he used to stand under the awning outside the entrance, breathing in the scent of wet timber.

On the bus, Heinrich realised just how tired he was. His shirt stuck to his back. At home he'd have a quick lie-down and then prepare a simple meal. He'd bought asparagus at the market and there was some ham in the fridge. There was still not a cloud in the sky. The constellations would shine brightly tonight.

She recognised him at once. Her heart missed a beat. Johanna Egger was covering a night shift for a colleague with a sick child and leaned over the body. There was blood on Heinrich Kienzl's face. She also noticed a big bruise. He'd taken a nasty tumble, hitting his temple on the bannister or on some other blunt object — the edge of the table or the stone kitchen floor, the various options flashed through her mind. His pulse was weak. He was unconscious, in what looked like a very deep sleep. For a split second, she thought she might faint, but she managed to hold onto something just in time. She needed to send him to another ward, through the swing doors, into the lift up to the fifth floor. Instead, she cradled his face in her hands.

Summer

He'd learned to swim with squashes: green *Flaschenkürbisse*. Or *Pitterlen*, as the butternut squashes are referred to in the local dialect. They'd been dried. Klaus Mair, six years old and with short, spiky blond hair, had picked them with his father in the garden. Some of the gourds were bigger than he was.

It was the summer of 1936, the end of the summer of an innocent year. It was September, but still warm and bright. The whole Mair family — his mother and father, his brother and two sisters, and himself — had been sleeping with the windows open for the past four months, with the sounds of crickets and cicadas drifting in through the windows and lulling them to sleep.

In the morning, the sunlight was so intense that Klaus would open his eyes beneath the sheets. And then he'd pretend he wasn't awake yet, not here anyway, but elsewhere, in a dream, in a fairytale forest of light.

The mornings in September were less dazzling than those in August, but otherwise there was very little to suggest that summer was coming to a close. The days were balmy and everyone was thirsty all the time. The noises of children playing in the water could be heard until late. His brother and sisters could swim, just like their friends, who all lived in the village by the lake as well. Screaming, they'd jump off a rock or swing from a branch into the Montiggler See. The boys would push the girls under the water. Little Klaus would just sit by the water's edge. He couldn't stay afloat. The water wouldn't carry him.

At the start of summer he'd tried, egged on by his sisters.

'Jump!' Helene and Renate had shouted. 'Go on, Klaus, jump!'

He'd been too scared and had waded into the water instead, deeper and deeper, until his feet no longer touched the bottom. He moved his arms and legs the way he'd seen the others do, but didn't manage to stay afloat. The underwater world, murky and pale green, flashed briefly before his eyes, until he was pulled up. Holding him tight, his sisters swam back to the shore. Klaus clambered up the bank, from where he watched the water-based fun: the jumping and the diving, the glistening columns of water spurting into the air. He cried, but nobody noticed.

Further attempts followed. Klaus tried to swim on his side, on his back, holding onto a branch or a tree stump. He thrashed about and swallowed water. The lake refused to keep him afloat.

'You're quiet today,' his father observed at lunchtime.

Klaus didn't react. They were sitting outside, at the long wooden table, six plates with home-grown beans in front of them. Perhaps the garden displayed the clearest signs of the end of summer. Dark purple figs lay scattered in the grass.

'He can't swim,' said Helene, the younger of the two sisters. 'He just can't do it.'

Klaus stabbed as many beans as he could with his fork and shovelled them into his mouth. Tears rolled down his cheeks, one after another.

When the meal was over, his father took him down to the basement, the darkest and coolest place in the house. On the back wall were shelves stacked with dozens of small jam jars: apricot, plum, raspberry, rosehip. Klaus had helped his mother with the apricot jam. While his sisters and brother were swimming in the lake, he'd removed the stones from the fruit. The sadness had been dispelled by the aroma of melting sugar.

'Let's carry the smallest ones upstairs,' his father said.

They were standing in front of a shelf with butternut squashes. Klaus had picked them the previous autumn, together with his father and brother. His mother had used the first few gourds to make creamy soup. Soup was another harbinger, a sign that one season was ending and another beginning. But for a six-year-old child, time passes imperceptibly. The squashes that didn't end up in deep plates were dried in the sun and stored in the cellar. They sounded hollow when you tapped them.

Klaus picked up the smallest butternut squash with both hands, while his father carried a slightly bigger one upstairs. And that's how they walked to the lake a little later, down the winding, narrow path through the forest. Father and son, *Pitterlen* under their arms.

'Daddy,' Klaus asked. 'Will the water keep me afloat now?'

'Yes, this time it will.'

'I've never seen anyone with squashes in the water.'

'Your dad learned to swim with them when he was a boy.'

In the same way that his own father had once tied squashes to his son's torso, Alfons Mair now tied them to Klaus's upper body on the shores of the Montiggler See.

They entered the water together, step by step by step. At some point, his feet no longer touched the bottom, and Klaus could feel himself lifting free and floating. He laughed. He couldn't believe it. The lake was keeping him afloat!

It was as if summer began all over again; as if now, finally, it poured its golden glow all over Klaus and he saw its true nature for the first time. He swam towards the other children, screaming with joy, splashing and kicking, and at the end of the day he pushed a girl under the water: Evi Hofer. She had dark, gleaming eyes, long hair, and skin as pale as white pebbles.

Klaus walked her back home, up the winding path through the forest, along the cobblestone street. He was carrying the bigger squash, Evi the smaller one. She lived three hundred metres down the road. Her mother was the most beautiful woman in the village. The baker trembled every time he served her.

'See you tomorrow,' Klaus said when he stood in front of his house.

'See you tomorrow,' Evi replied, and waved at him.

The following morning, Klaus and his brother and sisters passed the squashes between them as they walked to the lake together. By the shore, he waited for Evi. He waited with the gourds tied around his upper body. It was an image she'd never forget.

Hand in hand, they jumped into the lake. They spent their time chasing each other, spitting jets of water up into the air, and swimming to the far side with the others — the others to whom he now belonged, who were now his friends. By the time they reached the shore, they were exhausted, and lay in the sun like lizards. But only seconds later, they leapt back into the water. There were competitions to see who was the fastest, who could stay underwater the longest, and who could produce the loudest splash. Groups were formed: the girls against the boys. There was pushing and pulling, and everywhere Klaus looked water splashed up in the air, creating shimmery curtains, dripping rainbows. When Evi yelled his name, the sound reverberated endlessly in the lingering light.

At the end of the day, they ate figs on a toppled tree trunk. Their cheeks were red, their fingers sticky. The lake was as smooth as a pebble.

All the summers merged into one. All of his childhood summers, all of his friends' summers, they became one big melting pot of warm weather, water, and sweet fruit. Klaus saw it happen when he was old enough to see time pass, when time split his life in two, and he realised that some was ahead and some behind him.

Klaus Mair, sixteen years old and with straight dark hair, was packed off to the vocational school in Bozen by his father. He now spent one day a week in school, the other five in an engineering workshop. Those days were full of screeching machines, flashing metal, and filings. His hands were black. He made constructions for hangars, farming machinery, and ski lifts. In the evenings, he was so tired he went straight to bed after dinner. He shared a dormitory with a bunch of other lads. Some were bench fitters, like him, while others were training to be mechanics, plumbers, or blacksmiths. They all had black hands, too, but nobody spoke to him. He was alone again.

On Saturday afternoons, he walked home and devoured huge quantities of food. Sometimes his mother refilled his plate no fewer than three times. It was the hard work and the long walk, not to mention the fresh produce from the garden: kohlrabi, carrots, squashes, aubergines, beans, sprouts, cauliflower, broccoli, and courgettes. Every year, his mother would draw up a plan for the garden in a small notepad, outlining which vegetables — and which flowers, herbs, and berries — would go where. She loved her garden like she loved her family. At the end of every autumn, she wrapped paper bags around the sprouts so they could still be eaten in winter. She buried eggshells around the roots of the brassicas and used ashes as compost for the spring onions. Old leather soles were soaked in rainwater and the resulting liquid was used for irrigating her most precious plants. She knew which week was best for sowing and what day to fold over the onion tops. The rosebush was more than fifty years old.

On Mondays, Klaus got up at the crack of dawn to walk back to Bozen. More often than not it was still dark, even in summer. Inside the workshop, his eyes had to get used to the light. He was no longer a child;

his childhood was behind him.

The others were working, too — his friends from the neighbourhood, his brother and sisters. Helene was working as a shop assistant and Renate was a housekeeper for a family in Eppan. His brother helped his father in the apple orchard. As the eldest son, he was expected to take over the business.

Time, the ocean of time, was rolling on and was unstoppable.

His father was the first to die. It began innocently enough: a rash in his neck, the occasional headache in the evening. Then one day he couldn't get out of bed. The doctor attended to him and wiped the sweat from his forehead. Prayers were said. The family fed him creamy soup and lengthened his life by two days.

Klaus made an iron cross. His mother laid dahlias from the garden on his grave — the dahlias she loved so dearly because they flower for so long.

His sisters got married. Their husbands were lanky men, farmers from across the valley. They had children with strong teeth and white-blond hair. Klaus was named godfather of one of the girls and he taught her the sounds of the woodland animals.

He remained alone. He'd moved to Bozen and now worked at the plant where he'd started as a youngster. After all these years, he could no longer get his hands clean under the tap. Lunchtimes were spent in a canteen with a hundred other men; in the evenings he ate smoked bacon and gherkins in his own kitchen. He relished the silence, the absence of men and machines. The only thing he missed was his mother's garden.

Fate brought him back home. While walking the road between Kaltern and Eppan, his brother was hit by a truck. The driver hadn't seen him. It was a summer's day, shortly before the green-and-red Gravenstein was due to be harvested. His brother didn't recover from his injuries. For three days and two nights, he suffered the most excruciating pain. Then he lost his life, the cicadas lulling him to sleep for good.

Now it was up to Klaus to take care of the business. Picking red, yellow, and green apples with his black hands, he filled large wooden crates and took them to the fruit association. Twenty journeys a day, with the sun blazing over his head. The sound of children swimming and playing in the lake could be heard until late.

Since it was just the two of them now, his mother allotted less space to vegetables in her notepad. The empty spaces were filled with the names of flowers: asters, lilies, hydrangeas, gladioli, poppies, cornflowers, lady's smock, and sunflowers. In March, they were sown and fertilised with chicken manure. Two months later, his mother carried the first bouquet from the garden to the cemetery. Every week, she put new flowers on the graves of both her husband and son.

And so time passed, leaving more and more of itself behind Klaus. His pace slackened and his hair turned grey. The only person he ever spoke with was his mother. She talked to him about the garden, about what to sow and when, which herbs needed chalky soil, and how to get rid of slugs. 'Use my tights to stake up top-heavy plants,' she advised.

She died on the day he was supposed to sow parsley, 13 June, Anthony of Padua's feast day.

Klaus placed a bunch of purple snapdragons on her grave.

The land was leased to two brothers from the village. They planted new apple varieties: Pink Lady, Rubens, Kanzi. Later, some of the land was used for wine-growing.

Meanwhile, Klaus looked after his mother's garden. He disassembled his parents' old bed and used the iron mesh base as a support for runner beans. The weeds, he tackled with broken roll-down shutters, which he put down for paths between the vegetable beds. In summer, he ate at the long wooden table.

The rosebush was almost a hundred years old.

Every once in a blue moon he'd walk over to the lake. It was always quite a challenge, since the path's many twists and turns wore him out. From a bench, he'd watch the children jump off rocks. He'd hear them laugh and scream as they had their competitions and fights. Water splashed up all over the place. A boy dunked a girl, just as he'd once done to Evi Hofer.

The Kohlern Hotel

He arrived at the hotel around nightfall. The roads were covered in snow, and his shoes and socks were wet. The receptionist didn't have to ask his name. Rogier van Zeeuwen had been coming to the Kohlern Hotel to celebrate Christmas in solitude for three decades now. The hotel was located high up in the mountains, next to a small church where the villagers gathered on Christmas Day: farmers in their Sunday best, their daughters negotiating the snow in heels.

He'd seen the place change from a family-run business to a hotel that was largely run by an Eastern European workforce. It was still owned by the Schrott family, though; a yellow Italian sports car occupied the best parking space. The grandson who was now in charge welcomed him ahead of his first dinner. They had the same brief conversation every year.

'Good evening, Herr Van Zeeuwen. We're thankful to have you with us again this Christmas. On behalf of our staff, I'd like to wish you a pleasant stay.'

'Thank you, sir.'

Rogier van Zeeuwen remembered a time when he addressed the grandson informally. The little boy had been crazy about fire engines and racing cars. In fact, Rogier had given him a model car once: a silver-coloured Mercedes-Benz 190SL from 1955.

It was all *sir* and *madam* now. There were no more easygoing interactions.

His hiking boots were waiting for him in his room. Years ago, he'd had them delivered to the hotel, and they were usually taken up by the chambermaid. Anna, her name was. That's all he knew about her; that's all she'd let slip. They were large, lumbering shoes, but they kept his feet dry and stopped him from slipping on the icy roads around the hotel. Rogier van Zeeuwen wore them five days a year. The rest of the time he walked around in Santonis. He'd worked in property. It had started with a warehouse on an industrial estate, but offices and homes soon followed. Limited partners didn't hesitate to shell out large sums of money for a share. Thanks to him, entire neighbourhoods had been erected. Nearly all of it had been sold. And although the holding still existed, the rents were now collected by an external contractor.

He went for a short walk in the snow. Somewhere in the distance, a dog barked, and further still, another dog responded. Rogier van Zeeuwen looked at the white meadows and the frozen gardens outside the farms. He'd never been to Kohlern in summer. It was beautiful, he'd been told: grey horses, grazing cows, silver drops hovering in the late afternoon sky when the grass was being irrigated.

Three hours later, he was having dinner. It was the evening before Christmas Eve and not all the tables were occupied. Tomorrow, the hotel would be full. Most of the guests were elderly couples, but there would be a few young families, too, with fathers trying their best not to lose their patience. Everybody always stared.

Everybody stared at him, too. The first year, they would have seen a self-assured young man, tall and handsome, with dark blond, slicked-back hair. There was something enigmatic about him, elusive. Who spends Christmas alone in a hotel in the mountains? For ten years, they would have seen the same man, the waiters, the other guests, the elegant families who came to dine on Christmas Day. They would have seen an impeccably dressed gentleman, his hair gleaming in the candlelight. Then, gradually, the youthfulness faded; first it left his way of walking, then his cheeks, and finally his eyes. That's when people started seeing something else, too:

loneliness. Now it was all they saw.

He ordered Franz Haas, Manna 2007. *Manna* was the pet name of the winemaker's wife, the sommelier had told him in a whisper, as if sharing a secret. He'd instantly forgotten the grape varieties — he wasn't interested in details. Likewise, he'd always had staff take care of the small print in participation agreements.

It was an excellent white wine, but he used to enjoy it more. He thought back to bygone evenings in other countries, in big cities. Le Procope in Paris: enormous mirrors, chandeliers, polite conversation; joie de vivre and gorgeous women. He'd looked at their long legs while quaffing champagne and returned to his hotel with a woman ten years his junior. Rogier van Zeeuwen couldn't remember her name, but he did recall her skin, which was smooth beyond belief and almost luminous.

After dinner, he drank twelve-year-old Armagnac by the open fire. Every year, the bottle was ordered in especially for him: there were some things he still managed to get done, not with his looks, but with money. After three glasses, he headed back to his room. Noise could be heard behind one of the walls — a man's voice, a sudden yell, and then laughter. He walked to the window, and when he opened it the cold night flooded his room. Stars shone faintly in the sky. Something in his life had gone wrong, and it was too late to turn things around. It had nothing to do with the short days, or indeed winter. His thoughts had been dark and unrelenting for some time now, like weeds that keep coming back.

He knew it: he looked old, even though he wasn't. Or at least not ancient. Maybe the melancholic in him had finally surfaced — the grandpa he'd always been, deep down, which is why he'd seen things differently, at more of a remove, even at a young age.

He'd never been a cheerful child. 'Don't forget to smile,' his mother used to remind him, pinching his side. Over time he'd learned to be convivial, generous, and quick to laugh. As a result, his customers invited him to birthdays, and he got to attend second and third weddings abroad. Now the party was over, though; the lights had been extinguished. The silence was settling in, and he forgot to smile more and more often.

He was the first down for breakfast. The view was magnificent, with the mountains looking like a Caspar David Friedrich painting. Kitsch, almost. His espresso was served by a woman with dyed hair. Her face looked extremely young. He turned his head, watching her as she returned to the bar. But it was futile. He'd been expelled from Eden.

Outside, tiny snowflakes swirled through the air. He felt like sticking his tongue out, but was self-conscious.

It was quiet, and he was sure nobody could see him. Yet, with each step he felt the urge to look over his shoulder, to check if something was following him. An animal: a fox or a roe deer, perhaps. Not that he was scared. Rogier van Zeeuwen had never been scared. He knew the area; he knew which farm lay just around the corner and that he'd be greeted by barking dogs there.

Now and again he'd see faces behind a window: old women who were busy cooking. In fact, they were always up and about, doing something or other with a broom or an iron. In summer they'd be stooped over in the garden; in autumn they'd be tying bundles of kindling together with long branches. They retired at half-past eight in the evening and started the day before sunrise. Ageless women — that's to say, women whose ages he couldn't quite work out. What use was old age anyway, what was the point?

When the wind got up, Rogier van Zeeuwen turned around and walked back to the hotel. He skipped lunch, since there'd be a six-course meal in the evening. In his room, he tried to read a novel, but gave up after only a couple of pages. He'd never been much of a reader, and books were more of a performance for the outside world. He brought out a book in the hope that it would evoke some of the mystery that had surrounded him in the old days. Bulgakov makes a man more interesting, in the same way that a man who gifts model cars is liked better.

It was quiet in his room. Rogier van Zeeuwen was the only guest who was lying on his bed, staring at the ceiling. The hotel boasted a sauna as well as an outside whirlpool. The German guests went in naked, the Italians wore their swimming trunks or bikinis. There was something comical about it: two camps, poles apart.

He had never stood on the duckboard terrace stark naked, with steam billowing off him. That's just not the sort of man he was.

Halfway through a memory, he fell asleep. He had been thinking of a golden cornfield in Emilia-Romagna, bare feet, and in the distance, on top of a hill, the villa that once belonged to a prince of the House of Pignatelli.

During dinner, he observed a mother and daughter at the table next to him. He noticed the gulf between them, but both were trying hard to make it a pleasant evening. Their conversation dried up halfway through the second intermediate course: wild duck with beetroot. That's when a mobile phone appeared on the table. Every now and then the screen lit up, but the daughter didn't answer. The mother commented on other guests.

Rogier van Zeeuwen hadn't seen his daughters for more than fifteen years. Jolien, the eldest, had called him an arsehole in a restaurant in Dordrecht. A few days later, he'd received a letter from his other daughter. She didn't want to talk to him ever again.

He'd left his first wife for an artist. At least, that's

how he introduced her to his friends. In reality, she'd graduated from art school two years earlier and had been unemployed since. But she was a classic beauty, with long, blonde curls, a wide forehead, and Tatar eyes. He bought a convertible and drove to France with her. It made him feel liberated. Her body in the afternoon, a bottle of Veuve Clicquot on the bedside table — heady days. He didn't think of the mess he'd left behind: his first wife at home with two young children, one barely three years old and the other, eight months.

His marriage to the artist didn't last long. It had been a mistake to marry her so quickly, so impulsively. It was an episode, the first of many, except the rest would be without weddings. Rogier van Zeeuwen bought and sold business premises, and kept expanding with limited companies, sister companies in Ireland and Germany, a holding in Panama. He flew long-haul regularly, and spent little time at home. Sure, every now and then he forgot to smile, but those were fleeting moments in a sea of time.

'Don't you ever long for peace and quiet?' his first wife had asked him. They were having lunch in a brasserie, talking about things without a lawyer present. That was possible again. Jolien was off to university. He looked at his ex-wife. Beauty was a ship sailing away from her. But she'd weathered the storm. 'Wouldn't you like some peace and quiet?' she asked a second time.

Maybe that was the difference between men and women: men can't accept that they only live once.

Christmas was the only time of the year he withdrew. The crowded shopping streets, the atmosphere of goodwill and harmony — he couldn't stand any of it. He also felt detached from all the paraphernalia: the Christmas trees, the stars, the silver angels. At the Kohlern Hotel, only the waiters wished him a merry Christmas. It was done without a smile, cordiality Eastern European style. Rogier van Zeeuwen tipped them lavishly.

He was still generous, although he no longer saw the point of it. The weeds were shooting up all over the place. Suddenly he couldn't see himself travelling back to the valley, back home, his home. He could picture it — the white bricks showing through the bare branches, the dark blue shutters, the gravel on the garden path — but his thoughts swamped everything, not only his property, but also the cars in the garage, the catamaran he could take out to sea, and even his smaller possessions: the sofa, the TV, the kettle.

The following morning, he was woken up by the church bells. Villagers were gathering in front of the entrance. The sky was blue, and children were making a snowman. A little later, singing could be heard in the church. *O come, all ye faithful, joyful and triumphant! O come ye,*

O come ye to Bethlehem! By then, Rogier van Zeeuwen was already walking along the icy path that wound its way through part of the forest and past the farms. Nobody was home. Only the dogs were barking.

The path led up, and he kept walking. His fingers were tingling since he wasn't wearing gloves, so every now and then he blew into his fists. It had to be gorgeous in summer: calves in the meadows, raspberries in the farmers' gardens. He'd even seen a swing dangling from a large tree.

Maybe he ought to head back. They'd seat this melancholic man beside the warm fire, serve him a glass of Armagnac, and then he'd be fine again. But no, he kept walking, on and on and on. The snow, which was as soft as foam, gradually deepened. There was that sense of being watched again; a gaze so strong it made him stagger. It felt as if he had a lifetime's worth of eyes on him: the beautiful, sparkling eyes seen at parties, the twinkling eyes; the bleary irises of intoxicated women; the look of betrayal in his wife's eyes; the green eyes of his personal assistant with Danish blood. They all watched him walk away.

He knew he'd be found; he'd be missed at dinner. They'd be able to track him in the snow, see the footprints left by the sturdy shoes that made sure he didn't slip.

The memory returned when he sat down. His trousers became wet, and he felt his legs and buttocks grow colder and colder. The sun was already setting. Up in the mountains, the winter days are shorter than anywhere else. But Rogier van Zeeuwen's mind was on the long days of summer: the summer of his first honeymoon, with the sun high above a cornfield somewhere in Emilia-Romagna. In the distance, the house on the hill. He could see them sitting up there, a man and a woman, their hands intertwined.

The temperature fell, the mountain tops disappeared. He tried not to be scared.

Vineyard

The dog's name was Stella. Paul Barendse had been given her twelve years ago by the winegrower. She was a bastard, her mother a Shepherd, her father's breed unknown. Even now, she'd still scamper off every so often, to chase a hare among the vines, or a roe deer in the surrounding woods. The lead would make a whooshing sound as it lengthened and tightened. When she couldn't go any further, Stella would jump up and bark at the creature. Paul was pretty sure that he'd go before her.

It was October and mild. The sky was blue, the afternoon sun warm. The end of the year seemed a long way off. As did the other end — the big one. His life had revolved around literature. He had more than ten novels, three short-story collections, a novella, and a bundle of essays to his name. His best-known titles —

reprinted every other year — still sold, but there was no new novel in the pipeline. Not that he didn't try. Some mornings he'd sit down at the small table in front of the window, looking out across the valley, the rising dew, and the apple orchards left and right of the river. His wrinkled hands with the smooth fingertips moved slowly across the keyboard. He'd describe the light over the mountains, the colours of the leaves on the pear trees, the children who once played beneath them. One hundred words, he'd write, sometimes a bit more. A paragraph would suddenly stop — a beginning without a follow-up. He was probably going on instinct.

In the evenings, he'd walk to a small church with Stella. The first stretch was uphill, along the sandy path between the vines. The grapes had been picked three weeks ago. Blauburgunder. The wine was mild, but its bouquet of cherry and oak was powerful. Every year the farmer gave him a jerrycan.

Paul sat down in the lingering autumn sun, to look at the light over the mountains before it disappeared. Stella lay down at his feet. She knew they'd be heading back home once the church spire was shrouded in dusk. As so often, Paul thought back to the time when he wrote every day, with his sleeves rolled up, young and self-assured.

When he lived in San Genesio, he wrote in the slaughterhouse. The butcher had let out a small space that wasn't being used. He wanted to go to work like the rest of the village: set off early in the morning, come home in the evening. He was keen to prove himself. His neighbour was a car mechanic whose hands were black. Other men were roofers, locksmiths, and bricklayers. He worked with his hands, too, but he didn't get them dirty. On his first day at the slaughterhouse, the butcher had walked into his room and asked, 'You're writing?' He could barely believe it. Writing was something abstract; it had nothing to do with work. Books were filled by the breath of ghosts.

He never heard the animals themselves, unlike the large hoists with the chains that were used to strip the cows' hides; the metal implements on the stone floor; the electric saw hanging from the ceiling; the bones. But he managed to write, usually with classical music, sometimes with both Mahler and hacking sounds in the background.

Stella stretched when Paul rose to his feet. He stood still for a moment and looked at the valley. He wondered if loving nightfall more than the dawn made a man morose. Even though Paul Barendse was a shadow of the man he used to be, he didn't brood. He had no regrets.

They walked back at a snail's pace. There was no need to hurry. Every once in a while, the dog quickened her step and then slowed down again, as if she realised there was no point in walking faster. She'd seen her owner grow older, not to mention slower and quieter. Back in the day, his voice could often be heard around the vineyard, and then she'd always run over at once. Now they were like an old couple stuck with each other.

The house came in sight — a farm with natural stone walls, about a metre thick. The animals had long gone. The small stable was used for storing firewood, and a fig tree grew through the window of the chicken coop. A broken tractor was parked underneath the house.

Paul had fallen for the farm at first sight. He remembered the climb up from the village where his girlfriend's parents lived. They were invited over by the family sitting outside, at a wooden table, with large glasses of lemonade. The flavour of mint and lemon was refreshing. A friendship developed: long evenings, the stars bright in the sky, conversations about the faraway places the man and woman had been to and about the life that didn't come to a standstill, that just moved in ever smaller circles.

The placenta of their first child was buried in the west-facing garden. On top of it they'd planted an apricot tree. The fruits were dark orange, with a reddish glow on the sunny side.

The rural lifestyle appealed to them. In summer, they house-sat when the family went up into the mountains. He'd water the vegetable garden in his underpants, while she picked tomatoes and laid the wooden table.

A photograph showed her against the backdrop of the hill behind the farm, tanned legs sticking out from under a pink dress, meadow flowers in her hand. She was exceptionally beautiful.

And here she was still, standing in the big kitchen-diner. It smelled of sauerkraut. She glanced over her shoulder and smiled. If he looked closely, he could see the cheeks of the girl she used to be, the girl he used to know. Coming up behind her, Paul looked at the pots and pans on the stove. In the old days he used to kiss her when he came home. But he'd only been away a moment. To be fair, these days he never really left home at all.

They'd met in their early twenties. He was temporarily living with a countess married to a Dutchman while working on his first book. She lived in Bozen and was training to be a nurse for premature infants. She'd laughed at his German when she heard him stutter at the baker's. He hadn't noticed. But fate gave him a second chance and brought them together at a party. He was alone, she noticed, perhaps lonely, too. He couldn't remember what he'd seen. In all likelihood, just a young woman with bare arms and legs.

The next day, they went to a café with high brick arches, where she taught him German. Her fingertips touched his face. He didn't understand what she saw in him. Later, he thought he realised what women saw in him: an illustrious life. That's to say, a life that was different from their own. By then, he was already living in Italy (*Italy* — he never said South Tyrol) and had made a name for himself in the Netherlands. He owned a spacious apartment and they had two small children: a boy they'd named after an American writer he admired, and a girl with the rusk-coloured shoulders of Lolita. He'd graced the covers of glossy magazines with ads for anti-wrinkle creams. The accompanying story was always the same: the man who lived a quiet life with his family in the mountains, an anonymous life among farmers and loggers; the father who threw his children up in the air in idyllic fields. Some men, it seems, can be in different worlds at once. He was one of them. In the Netherlands he was a rising star. He did readings and appeared on talk shows. They turned up wherever he went: young women in high heels; women who were freshly showered; women whose youth was a breath of fresh air in the small, grey rooms where he appeared; women in frayed jeans with a simple top. But there were also women wearing too much blush; women who were ten years his senior; women who found it hard to part with their beauty.

He hadn't forgotten the nights, but what he couldn't remember was how easy it had been, how little he'd had to do. He recalled a woman with long red hair. She lived with her young son. For six months, he kept his toothbrush in a beaker in their bathroom. He walked in and out of lives, the way some people get in and out of elevators. What had he been looking for? What had he found? Little, if anything. But the curiosity was insatiable. It was the longing for the unfamiliar, for the unknown and the transient. He was incapable of saying no — too weak, too cowardly. It was the absence of commitments, too: beauty, temptation, and nothing else. He was a dog and he knew it.

She was still here. It hadn't been easy. Irwin Shaw's wife could list her husband's mistresses in alphabetical order. His own wife didn't know any names or faces, but she was aware of their existence. A battalion of ghosts gathered around their bed when he came home after a trip.

Once, after overhearing snippets of a phone conversation with an actress, his wife had thrown him out. The words 'I want to see you, too' had made her physically sick. 'Out!' she'd shouted. 'Go to Holland and don't come back!'

He'd gone down on his knees to beg for forgiveness. In his diary, he jotted down the nights he spent in their son's bunkbed. In the mornings, the little head appeared above him: 'Why aren't you sleeping in Mama's bed?' The boy often snuggled up beside him for a while, and so he and his son would lie in one bedroom and his wife and daughter in the other. There was love, but it wasn't evenly distributed — or, at least, not the way it's meant to be.

Two years later, they split. He returned to the Netherlands. It was a dramatic farewell, rife with recriminations and yelling, with his daughter howling and his son pleading: 'Daddy, daddy … Dad!' Finally, the door was slammed shut.

Paul Barendse drank from the cup that wasn't his, the cup from which lesser men drank, those who were insatiable. He became arrogant and quarrelled with colleagues. For a while he lived with a philosophy student. She had long, blonde hair like a waterfall.

It had been a mistake — the biggest one of his life. It was a difficult thing to admit to himself. At first he thought the damage amounted to nothing but a book, a novel that wasn't being written. But that was a delusion. If he'd had friends, they'd have seen him sink. But he had no friends, no house, no wife. There were hotel rooms and addresses around town where he was welcome. There were restaurants with wooden flooring and tables by the window; parties to which he wore smart suits. And as always, there were the endless nights. He had everything, and he had nothing.

In literature, there's seldom a way back. He didn't believe in it himself, in the happy ending, the final major chord. But perhaps, for him, it was the only way. Paul Barendse had enjoyed a respectable upbringing. He simply lacked the talent for the big crash and burn.

In his absence, his daughter had shot up fourteen

centimetres. They all regarded him as a stranger, but he was welcome nonetheless. Picking things up again, winning back trust, was going to be a struggle, but he was prepared to fight. What had kept him and his wife together was still there. It was invisible, yet he could see it, feel it. She caressed his face with her fingertips. He lay next to her in bed, motionless, listening to her breathing. The first time he touched her, she cried. It was too early; it would take time.

And then the farm became available. The children of the family that lived there had left home, and now their parents wanted to go back to the city. It felt like yet another chance. Paul was won over at once.

His wife had reservations. 'Can you live here?' she asked.

'What do you mean?'

'Isn't it too quiet?'

He knew what she meant. Nothing ever happened here, except the changing of the seasons. He used to look down on the people in San Genesio for their mentality, and for their culture, too: the folksy music and the *Speckknödel*. Bacon dumplings, but no books, no violins. The local paper featured car crashes on its front page, with victims' names under a photo of the wreck. And wherever you went, people were yakking and gossiping in that appalling dialect his children spoke, too, and which had even crept into his own German.

Mazzon, the village the farm was in, was smaller than San Genesio. He wasn't sure if he could live here the way his wife meant — *forever*.

Still, he nodded. He was willing to give it a try.

'I'm always scared ...' his wife whispered, but didn't finish her sentence. She wrapped her arms around Paul and held him tight. In the hospital where she worked, babies were looked after in incubators. Some had knees the size of her little fingernail. There were parents who kept hearing the beeps of the monitors at home. She'd heard stories of mothers waking up in the middle of the night, at the exact moment their child passed away in the hospital.

Like so many men, Paul never knew what to say at moments like this. So he was silent, waiting for it to be over, really; for it to go away.

Their children, six and eight now, settled in quickly. They were familiar with the farm from their many weekend visits and summer holidays. Now it was their own patch: the fruit trees, the red poppy fields, the buzzing insects. They walked barefoot under the vines and climbed on each other's shoulders to reach the dark purple bunches. His wife and daughter made jam from the apricots, while he taught his son to chop wood. There was no warm water; in winter, the house was heated with large stone furnaces. A renovation would require a bestseller. He wrote the book at the small table in front of the window overlooking the valley. Sometimes he suddenly rose to his feet, as an almost feverish energy surged through his body. Then he'd stand in front of the window, the way Hemingway used to stand in front of the typewriter in his bedroom, not far from the Mexican Gulf. The words would pour onto the paper, five thousand in a single week.

There were times he was amazed at the enduring success, at the many opportunities that came his way. He feared something bad might happen to his children — the price for their carefree days. Or that he himself might fall ill with, say, cancer of the bone, and be given less than a month to live.

But fate had no interest in them. They appeared to be living in a bubble. In the evenings, they usually sat on the sofa with mugs of tea and watched television. One after the other, the children would fall asleep. He'd breathe in their scent and kiss their hair. Life didn't come to a standstill; they just moved in ever smaller circles. Life became a living room surrounded by a house with thick walls, and around it the land that ended at the winegrower's wooden fence. There didn't seem to be anything beyond that.

Summer was the most delightful season. The children looked after a donkey Paul had adopted from a nearby farm. There were vegetables from the garden, scarlet strawberries, and aromatic herbs. Huge sunflowers towered over everything. Lazy afternoons were spent in hammocks. Life was lived outdoors. They walked up and down the fields and washed their feet with the garden hose. They tackled the grass with scythes and rakes. The nights were splendid, punctuated in August by grotesque thunderstorms. Later came the harvest and the colours of autumn: the violet of figs and the rust of apples rotting away because nobody had picked them.

He still travelled back to the Netherlands, albeit less and less often. Paul Barendse was over forty now, and his blond hair was thinning. His books had a guaranteed first print run of tens of thousands of copies. Doors continued to open left, right, and centre, but he no longer had any business behind some. It was all too noisy, the people too young.

His mistress was a film producer. In Cannes, she'd slept with the great and the good. She told him long stories about them over breakfast. Among them were a famous British actor who'd wanted to take her in the press area bathroom, and a Russian director who offered her a role on the condition that she married him. She didn't always have time for Paul. The day would come, she said, when she'd stop answering his phone calls. This was a woman who'd left men because they'd bought her gifts.

In your mind you can be anywhere you want to be, but Paul was often in the big hotel by the pier. This is where, in the olden days, steamers set off for America.

The suites were former management offices, and still had the original carpets on the floors. The hearth contained a briquette of compressed wood that caught fire the second you held a match to it. In his memory, he stood in front of the tall windows overlooking the New Meuse, the river that had carried countless fortune seekers to the open sea. Her voice echoed through the bathroom, which was as long as a Cessna. 'Can you top up my glass?'

He thought of her body in the bath, the foam up to her breasts, the other men who didn't have her.

At home, the seasons came and went. His children began to read his books and recognise themselves in some of the stories, prompting his daughter to observe: 'But Mama never cried.'

He didn't know what to say to that, how much he could tell his children. In the small rooms where he read from his work and took questions from the audience afterwards, he tended to stumble over his answers, too. He denied any parallels between his life and work. He cited the American writer James Salter, who'd written a book about a couple with children growing apart. The author divorced his wife when the novel hit the shops. Salter, too, had asserted there were no parallels. No doubt his children knew better.

Paul's son reached the age at which he wanted to come along on trips to the Netherlands. They wouldn't see much of each other, meeting either in the dimly lit hotel room in the dead of night or at breakfast. Paul would be out a lot, so his son was given a key card and pocket money. He smelled the stink of cigarettes on the boy's clothes, but asked no questions. In turn, his son said nothing about the perfume that clung to his father when he lay down beside him.

Then came the reunion: the mornings they'd sit at the breakfast table in the kitchen together, his wife, his son and daughter, and Paul reading the paper. The tabletop would be covered in crumbs, while the coffee cooled down in small cups. A string quartet played on the radio. Life within the ancient walls of marriage. It wasn't a game, but that didn't mean you couldn't gamble it all away.

A sense of farewell suffused the air. They were moving towards it — and had done so for years, perhaps. There were little things, portents: the locked bathroom door in the morning, his daughter whispering on the phone. They were survivors, Paul realised, but they were no longer the same family. After the summer, his son would be going off to study in Bologna, at the oldest university in the world. His daughter, meanwhile, spent days on end in a bikini in the hammock. Paul had a feeling she was ripe for the picking.

His wife was afraid that he, too, would leave. It was only a matter of time, she figured. In the evening, as they held each other, he looked at the lines around her eyes.

One night — they'd only just gone to bed — he came out with it. He wanted to live in a city again, for a while anyway, maybe no more than a year.

'What?' she asked.

He explained that he didn't want to go on his own, but with her.

'What city? Not Amsterdam, I hope?' She had a horror of the Netherlands.

'Berlin,' he replied. 'Or else a city in Italy: Verona, Padua, Perugia.'

'We've never been to Perugia.'

'I want hustle and bustle, streets with people and cars in them, and bars where you can drink until the early hours.'

Quite unexpectedly, she moved closer and snuggled up against him. She listened to his heartbeat for a while.

'What about the farm?' she asked. 'What do you want to do about the farm?'

He ran his fingers through her grey hair. It had happened really fast. She'd decided not to dye it, and he'd never said anything about it. As for himself, he was scared stiff of going bald, like his father had been around sixty. His dad's hair had thinned until there was precious little left.

'Maybe we can find a tenant,' he said. 'Young people who love the countryside.'

That made her smile. Their daughter had now flown the nest, too. She'd recently moved in with an architect and lived on the seventh floor of an apartment building in Bozen. By two in the afternoon, the sun had all but disappeared from view.

Still, against the odds, they'd managed to find a young couple who wanted to rent their farm. The woman had sighed with pleasure on the first viewing. With her nose stuck in a rose, she'd exclaimed, 'Honey, smell this!' Paul felt a bit sorry for the husband.

'Isn't it too quiet?' the man asked, his question aimed at no one in particular.

There isn't much here, Paul was tempted to say — trees, vines, grass that reaches up to your knees in summer — but he kept his mouth shut. He let the young couple survey the small radius of action for themselves. This was all there was, but it would have to suffice. The author Paustovsky once wrote that you could spend your whole life on one and the same piece of land, and yet see an extraordinary amount.

They moved to Berlin and lived in Charlottenburg for fourteen months. He spent the mornings writing in the attic of their apartment, while his wife found a job at the Old National Gallery. In the afternoon, they roamed the streets and drank aperitifs in cafés with ramshackle tables and chairs. Berlin wasn't a rough diamond, but a piece of jewellery devoid of any gems.

A ransacked city. They talked about books they'd both read. When she disagreed with him, he raised his voice, sticking up for writers as if they were family. 'Joseph Roth isn't a misogynist! He's afraid of women!' In the U-Bahn they held hands. They slept peacefully in the city that never sleeps.

Autumn: the scent of roast chestnuts, the wide avenues of Prenzlauer Berg. Life was never perfect, but at times it was pretty good. They fed the pigeons near the water tower and walked in the pale, autumnal light, had dinners in crowded restaurants, and spent Sundays reading the paper. They thought of their children, who were both in other cities. Their son would be coming to visit at Christmas, while their daughter, who'd been invited by the architect's parents, would join them later. Together, they'd see in the new year.

His wife had forgotten the lights. The evenings in the country were dark, with not a single illuminated window to be seen. But here there were twinkling lights everywhere: in trees, on façades, draped over monuments. The streets were covered in a fine dusting of snow. The four of them walked across it, the women's hands in thick mittens. That evening, Paul said things that can only be said after alcohol. He was happy they were all together — him and his wife, the two of them with their children. He couldn't believe they were all grown up now.

'Dad,' his daughter said.

But he carried on. He loved them so much. They meant the world to him. He couldn't imagine life without them. Of course, he couldn't take any credit for it, he said. His children knew what he was going to say; they knew everything. The months, spread over many years, when the house was filled with sadness, the leaden silence alternating with slamming doors, and the mornings he'd woken up in his son's bunkbed — nothing had been forgotten, everything had slipped into the collective bloodstream. As teenagers they'd sworn they'd never get married.

What other men might say as a joke, at an anniversary or a leaving do, he said in all earnestness to his wife, straight from the heart. He thanked her for not walking out on him.

He raised his glass. It was an awkward moment, and too early to boot. It wasn't yet midnight. But that didn't stop them from raising a toast to the year ahead, blank as a sheet of paper, and full of promises for those who were young.

At midnight, they watched the fireworks over the city. Soon afterwards, his children went out into the street, leaving the two of them behind, surrounded by uncorked bottles and glasses with a few last drops. He was afraid to speak; he'd already said too much this evening.

In bed, they listened to the last rockets exploding in the sky over Berlin. The lights had gone out.

'Are you asleep?' she asked eventually.

'No.'

'What are you thinking of?'

He was thinking of the fourteen centimetres his daughter had grown in his absence. At times, sitting at his desk, he'd indicated the length to himself with his index fingers.

'Why?' he asked after a while. 'Why did you never leave me?'

She was strong, she was brave, she'd have managed on her own — on her own with two children, that is.

He felt her body coming closer. She whispered something in his ear, words he'd never written down; words that didn't work on paper. But in the early hours of New Year's Day they would do; they were fine.

They were still going. He sat opposite her at the large kitchen table. His wife took small bites, he drank a glass of Blauburgunder with his meal. The silence: there was the cutting of the tender sausage, the waiting for the other to finish eating. He always cleared his plate first.

Outside, the sky wasn't completely dark yet. Over the years they'd started eating earlier, sleeping earlier, the elderly couple stuck with each other. There were grandchildren: two boys, brothers, and a girl who was their son's daughter. Their portraits hung in the hallway. One of the grandsons resembled him. Looking at the boy, he saw himself: the same cold blue eyes, rolled-up sleeves in summer, and self-assurance.

They'd lived on the coast for a few years. A decade after Berlin, it was to be their final adventure. It had been his idea to go to Sicily and rent a house by the beach, just south of Noto, where the sea is green and blue; where there is space, a horizon of sky and water, and seasons that differ from those in the north. Giuseppe Tomasi di Lampedusa once wrote that summer in Sicily lasted six months. But the sea was refreshing. Wearing little more than boxer shorts on the hottest days, Paul wrote on a laptop with sand between the keys, with the sound of the waves in the background, and his wife a tiny dot somewhere on the beach. There were still readers who were waiting for a new book filled by his breath.

Then the circle closed again, and they had to make do with the small piece of land that belonged to them. When Paul's wife saw him decline, faster than herself, she forced him to come for a walk with her every morning. On their return home, they had breakfast together and then he sat down at his writing table. Later, the dog arrived, and the three of them would go out walking together.

He wrote one more book. Then he called it a day. What was the point in sitting in the same chair for hours on end? Other writers had arrived on the scene, others had taken his place in the pantheon. Still, his books were on the school curriculum, and his collected works had been published. Their children visited regularly. He saw them watching him, checking to see if he remembered to do up his fly.

The dog died at the end of autumn. The ground was already hard. Paul needed an entire morning to dig a grave under the fig tree, the shaded spot where Stella had whiled away many hours of her life. The first few days after her death, he was sad, but then the heaviness lifted, as if his heart simply lacked the strength to carry on mourning.

Now it was just the two of them going on their walks. The villagers saw them without a dog, as did the hares. Perhaps some of them were puzzled, looking around nervously to see where Stella had gone. But everything was peaceful — no taut lead, no barking, only an elderly couple strolling through the vineyard, inching towards the red dawn that heralded winter. He knew she was no longer afraid. One day he'd be gone, but they'd meet again, buried side by side. The glare of the sun absorbed all the colours around them, and their shadows were dozens of metres long. He paused and looked at the trees, the vines, and the short grass.

His wife had walked on, but now retraced her steps.

'What's the matter?' she asked.

He was unable to formulate an answer, to explain what he saw. It had to do with the light and with the familiarity of everything around him. Somehow he still felt that every day offered him a new chance. His wife took his hand, and together they looked at what had been around them all this time. Standing there, on the sandy path among the vines, old together, it was almost too good to be true. But it was true.

All but one of Gustav Mahler's symphonies end on a major chord. They walked on, illuminated by the strengthening sunlight coming from above the mountain tops. He'd never really known whether he could live here. But now he knew he could die here.

Acknowledgements

I owe a debt of gratitude to Karl and Nikolaus Schmid. Not only did they answer all of my questions, but they also took the time to tell me about the history of the apple harvest. In addition, I have drawn on the following sources: *Südtirol. Vom Ersten Weltkrieg bis zur Gegenwart* [*South Tyrol: from World War I to the present*], Rolf Steininger, StudienVerlag, Innsbruck, and *Farbe & Qualität der Südtiroler Apfelsorten* [*Colour and Quality of the South Tyrolean Apple Varieties*], Kurt Werth, Verband der Südtiroler Obstgenossenschaften GmbH.